An Anthropology of the Subject

Holographic Worldview in New Guinea and Its Meaning and Significance for the World of Anthropology

Roy Wagner

UNIVERSITY OF CALIFORNIA PRESS

Berkeley / Los Angeles / London

This book is a print-on-demand volume. It is manufactured using toner in place of ink. Type and images may be less sharp than the same material seen in traditionally printed University of California Press editions.

University of California Press
Berkeley and Los Angeles, California

University of California Press, Ltd.
London, England

Library of Congress Cataloging-in-Publication Data
Wagner, Roy.
    An anthropology of the subject : holographic worldview in
    New Guinea and its meaning and significance for the world of
    anthropology / Roy Wagner.
        p.   cm.
    Includes bibliographical references and index.
    ISBN 978-0-520-22587-9 (pbk. : alk. paper)
    1. Anthropology—Philosophy.   I. Title.
GN33.W28   2001
301'.01—dc21   00-061991
                                                                      CIP

Printed in the United States of America

The paper used in this publication meets the minimum requirements
of ANSI/NISO Z39.48-1992 (R 1997) (*Permanence of Paper*).♾

An Anthropology of the Subject

To Aubrey and Dagiwe, to Dawn, Smokey, and "Mother" Wright

To
Marcella

R. Merritt Johnson
5/8/11

The Dreamist

R. Neville Johnston

authorHOUSE®

AuthorHouse™
1663 Liberty Drive
Bloomington, IN 47403
www.authorhouse.com
Phone: 1-800-839-8640

First published by AuthorHouse 1/3/2011

ISBN: 978-1-4567-0036-2 (sc)
ISBN: 978-1-4567-0037-9 (e)
ISBN: 978-1-4567-0035-5 (dj)

Library of Congress Control Number: 2010916802

Printed in the United States of America

This book is printed on acid-free paper.

Certain stock imagery © *Thinkstock.*

Table of Contents

Chapter One

The time is 7:59 PM, the date is equivalent to October 10, 2097. Silence has been called for in the enormous Dream Dome auditorium. The greatest viewing audience in the history of broadcasting is standing by, and all for a show called The Dreamist.

Tonight, six contestants, will compete to be recognized as the world's greatest dreamer. Tonight, someone will be given the very prestigious title of "Dreamist." A waking Master of Ceremonies called Runger, hosts the show. He has a peculiar habit of always referring to himself in third person. As in, "The Runger," as he likes to call himself. The show is regulated by panel of officials, a group of Doctors and a number of former Champions of the show, the Dreamists.

The basic rules are quite simple. If the dream character you are projecting is killed, you may transmute into something else, but in order to do this, you have to be on your home territory on the gigantic stage. Of course, you may leave the contest by choice, at any time. If for any reason you awaken, you're out. The last person sleeping wins.

The broadcast will continue until there is an official winner. The record for length of show, to date, is 99 hours, 37 minutes, 14 seconds and 2 pixations. It has been estimated that about thirty five trillion marbles (units of currency) changed accounts in the betting that ensued during that particular broadcast.

An entire generation has grown up on this show. In the early days the broadcasts were chaotic. Equipment failure was common. The show could be held up for hours on just simple glitches. The first and second generations of computers could misinterpret data and attempt to project things that cannot exist third dimension, at least not for very long.

Once the show began to train its own dreamers, it was all different. Shortly there after they went the whole distance. Dreamist founded its own school, Integrating Astral Matrix University. They offer any number of degrees including Doctorate of Multidimensional Dreaming. People go to school for 8 years just to be able to apply, to be on this show.

Not all who apply are accepted. It's really more in the neighborhood of one ninth of one percent of the entire enrollment of the school that ever gets to see the stage from the contestant's point of view.

The audition, or finals as the students call them, stretch over a year. Even then, once you have qualified, you just get on the list and may wait years before getting your chance to actually be on the show. Still thousands line up.

The Dream Dome was built to accommodate, exclusively, this show. There are a quarter million seats surrounding an enormous circular stage. This is small by current population standards. The platform is inlaid with a holomatrix grid. It's in the form of a circle, divided into six equal pieces, each called a petal. Around it are six sleep chambers, called IG-wooms with the contestant already bedded down within, asleep, before the show goes on the air.

Each sleep chamber has a team of twenty-one highly qualified technicians, doctors, a personal coach and two officials who monitor the whole operation and of course, its sleeping contestant. This team has the authority to yank a player, if they feel the person could be hurt.

They are wired into the most sophisticated holographic projection system known to man. Their dreams will be projected onto the stage, in truly vivid colors and certainly larger than life.

There have been thirty-three deaths, and one hundred and sixty-four people permanently, mentally disabled, in the history of the Dreamist. One hundred and thirty nine of the disabled never again awoke, and were therefore eventually disqualified. Twenty-five never again went to sleep, but technically are conscious or at least semi-conscious. It's something like coma-lite.

All of these injured contestants live, it's just nobody knows exactly where. What has happened to them is and endless source of intellectual tattle-prattle, ongoing in the media. No one knows. Will tonight's show include the next fatality, will tonight's show include the next mind melt?

Chapter Two

The crowd hushes as announcer opens the show. "The Runger says, Welcome, to the two thousand, and sixty first broadcast of "DREAMIST!" As we all know, the motto of this show is..."

Two hundred and fifty-thousand voices chant the apothegm in perfect unison: "Before it can be, it must first be dreamed!" This is followed by exalted cries, wild cheering, the audience is exuberant.

The Runger continues, "Tonight's show is special. We have accepted a contestant that didn't graduate from our University. You might call her a "natural." She has had some training though... She held a general's rank during the years of the dreaming wars. The Runger knows what an honor it is, to introduce a name, that we are all quite familiar with, Kabel Newstarr."

A current of energy surges through the audience. There has long been the custom of bringing something, anything that makes noise to express the spirit, the adulation that the crowd feels. Horns, sirens loud popping sounds and not to mention the traditional applause floods the air.

Throughout the Dream Dome, the walls are gigantic television panels, called 4DV. This latest generation of television technology doesn't just show scenes, it's like you actually experience them. They begin to "show" pictures of General Newstarr. Her decorations, her history in the wars, the dream lab she and her troops used in combat, (all primitive by "Dreamist" standards.) Finally moments of her personal history all unfold rapidly, as though what one might see, if one's life were flashing before their eyes just prior to death.

The general herself was unaware of all of this going on. In the IG-woom she is resting comfortably, in fact very little cerebral activity. An excellent sign, her team is pleased. This indicates an inner calm, a centeredness in her dreamtime. Let's call it a dreaming confidence, no butterflies.

The Runger speaks again, "Kabel you may manifest your dream body now..." This time Newstarr hears the voice in her sleep and all the monitors in her IG begin to increase their readings.

The first dream body of the evening begins to take shape. It starts in the center of the stage. The air becomes "thick." Torrents of lighter and darker, lighter and darker, dense and less dense, revolve by each other, like smoke swirling over a hot lamp. Finally, a dot of light appears, just one. Then another, then more, they begin to mass, forming into a swirl of luminal bubbles. They are all different colors. Filaments begin to form. All of it, whirling higher and higher, gaining more and more mass, until suddenly it all just drops, into a form.

The audience can't quite make it out. There is obviously a huge mass. The creature is black in color, making it even more difficult to discern. It is accompanied by a deep musky scent. The creature begins to pull itself erect. There is a startled gasp from the crowd. It's an enormous black bear, rising majestically. It stands, stretching ten feet in the air. Weighing in at over twelve hundred pounds, she's a female, said to be the far deadlier of the two genders. The dreamer dreams her arms raising, flashing the claws. As she stretches to her height she lets out a roar.

This is no ordinary roar, it has been enhanced. It's above a hundred and thirty five decibels, just below the legal level for the show. The sound lays low, all between bass C, all the way up to D flat. It is designed to, and it does, shake the very base of our primordial fear.

The audience goes absolutely silent. For a moment each individual freezes. Each individual body reverts to its survival mode. As in, "If I'm perfectly still, she won't see me." Perhaps a minute went by, perhaps more. Finally someone laughs and everyone resumes breathing.

Her call has had another affect. It set in motion a second set of twin swirls. The audience becomes confused. Is this the next contestant? Every eye studies this "phenomenon," that is whirling around.

The two begin to revolve around the behemoth, drawing more and more mass. One positioned on each side of her. They balance in the rotations, like Deimos and Phobos around Mars. She raises her head straight up, and begins to turn clockwise, the opposite of the way the little "tornadoes" are moving. If she weren't so imposing she would resemble a bear dancing in a circus.

A massive flash of light punctuates itself with rolling thunder. The sound wave brakes across the theater. Just as before, the two new energy fields just drop into form. Twin bear cubs, each one weighing in, at around six hundred pounds. This is more than a ton of bear. The sight of the three is astounding. That someone would think of inhabiting three dream bodies at once, is to say the least, magnatudinous! This is precedent setting!

The two join their mother, and the family goes to their place at the center of the first petal. The applause is deafening, as the three take a bow simultaneously.

As the adulation of the crowd dies down, the master of ceremonies resumes announcing. "All right, The Runger Says, our second contestant is Stella Orion, from right here in Paraguay. She graduated third in her class at the Dreamist University. She says that after collecting the prize marbles she will set up practice as a Dream counselor in Brisbane Australia. There, she can also peruse her hobby of underwater Archeology. As you know there was recently discovered, some fifty thousand year old ruins from the so called "Monkey Civilization." So far the largest skull found has a capacity of only twelve hundred c.c.s of brain space. The average adult on Earth today has a cerebral capacity of eighteen hundred and sixty seven.

Stella is engaged to, Todd Beauen, a graduate of the Institute for the Study of Temporal Anomalies. Todd is continuing to train to be one of the first true Chrononauts.

The stream of pictures fade from the viewers as the as the announcer speaks, "The Runger says, Stella, please convene your dreaming body."

Something sparkles in the very center of the stage about seven feet in the air. The audience comes to attention. What unfolds next is an exquisite ballet of color, sparkle, and luminescence. It spins more rapidly gaining light with each rotation. Finally it pulses an enormous flash of yellow light.

The pulse leaves a delicately shaped ellipse of light surrounding the original luminal axis. It's like a gossamer statue. The spin continues, there is more and more light folding into the equation. Soon, this elliptical mass appears to solidify. Its rotation slows and finally stops. The surface is covered with concentric stripes of yellow and black resembling a bee or yellow jacket. The movement comes to a complete halt. It just stands there, upright balanced. Not a word has been said, not a single sound.

Shrieks come from the audience as long ragged slits appear about where the heart would be. Something quite sharp, flesh? It's some kind of finger, how could it make a sound like a scissor. It's an insect, its exoskeleton, tears its way through its cocoon. Thus the creature is born, revealing it's elegantly designed insectoid body. Imagine a body made up of hydraulic equipment. What power, what an unusual approach to building a dreaming body.

The head is equipped with a very sophisticated "Antenna." They measure heart rate, temperature, thousands of things in the environment the other contestants may not be aware of. The eyes are designed to function in a much wider electromagnetic spectrum than ours are. More than anything, it resembles a giant grasshopper. And like a grasshopper, it's capable of spitting caustic fluids.

The creature takes its bow, but this time, to a series of boos and cat calls. Recent insect infestation had affected food supplies in this part of the planet so an insect is not really a politically correct choice. However, Stella knows this and intends to take advantage of the psychological impact. It's a well-known fact, that the more you hate someone, the more you give up your power to them. She takes her place in the center of her triangular home territory on the game board.

The Runger speaks, "Contestant number three is Mendel Allay. He graduated fifteen years ago. Just last year he put in his request to audition for our show. He has been off planet working at the IO Colony monitoring the psychological effect on dreaming that colony assignments have on us, as well as the differences in the dreaming index, of those born on colony."

The 4DV panels light up with pictures of Mendel on colony. Jupiter is cutting an arc through the inner stellar sky in the background. Next are shots of his dream lab, the crew he works with out there, he and his dog playing. Pets are always a good thing. Next, copies of the books he has written appear, then finally his statement of intent, if he wins.

"Upon his return to Earth, Mendel, qualified in a record ten months and joins us tonight as..."

The whole audience focuses its attention of that first glimmer. This time, not such a bright light. Its movement is simply, spin. First forming a shaft of light, then it begins gradually bending and transmuting, apparently effortlessly, into a spiral of matter. It's a light purple peach color with a bright blue halo. The mass increasing, it fills itself out into an egg shape.

Still revolving slowly coming to rest, an enormous gelatinous mass comes into being. Still blue, egg shaped and becoming gradually more and more transparent. As though millions of little parts are finding their places, and as they do, so the articulation clears, becoming transparent.

Again the crowd is silent. Without a sound this mass gently settles into the form of a gigantic teardrop. Perfectly formed, glistening, it stands nine feet tall. There is a spontaneous applause. It's a magnificence to behold. Who could have imagined such a dream body?

The audience is beside itself with delight. They make such a loud and jubilant noise. Picture thousands of howler monkeys, with little tiny air horns. Now add in alcohol and free food. Now add evocatively clad female monkeys encouraging this behavior. Now multiply by ten and ten again. Now we are approximating the quarter million population response.

"Right now were going to take a break and The Runger, is gonna tell ya about what our other World Dreamists have been up to, and then well be back, to introduce our three other contestants...

Physicist Dr. Nigel Boyd, got every body's favorite wish. He experienced his 4th dream visit from Dr. Ming. Dr. Ming is a Dreamist from the year 2160. Dr. Boyd, as you may remember, was given the Nobel Laureate in Magnatronics. Has been elected, Head Chair of the University of Bombay, Research Laboratory. This is the facility where we are building a faster than light engine.

Dreamist Dr. Ming, has returned here in our time to talk

to Dr. Boyd about light technology. Nigel says, 'We just sit and have tea and then in the morning I have the most interesting new ideas about the designing. I look forward to the time that I can dream this powerfully.' The Runger says, visits from these advanced dream teachers are always such a joy.

Dreamist Sangik Gibson is announcing the release of his new book. This is the twelfth in his series of mystery novels. Those of us following this delightful game, know that this next book is the last book and contains the final piece of the puzzle. With it the Greater Mystery can be solved. As well you know, there are 100 billion marbles for anyone who can put all those pieces together.

Member of Parliament, Sir Elroy Flint, announced that he has shared dreamtime with, none other than the 2077 Dreamist, Chief Six Fingers. Elroy says the Cherokee Chief and he, have had a powwow and that he is changing his vote, in favor of the Eight Ocean bill. This bill will fund the creation of a "Lake" to be formed in the Pacific Ocean."

The torrent of information running through the walls switches to photos of Clue Houstrum, the 2070 winner. Magnificent is she. The tall hermaphrodite has been very popular in the media lately because of her plans to actually create the idea of Nikola Tesla's to a put 33 story "antenna" on the North and South poles. If this were done, there would be zero square inches of places, on this Earth, that you could not get, holo transmission and electric power.

On the screens all sorts of diagrams, projections, Satellite recon data flows by. This would also allow us a much greater range of abilities as far as deep space transmission. Ships at enormous distance can receive a far more sophisticated data stream. Our planet will be able to communicate with the galactic government, unassisted, for the first time. It will be a triumph of mankind.

This footage was apparently taken just moments ago. Clue Houstrum, is addressing the Royal Family in China in the Forbidden City. She simply stops, right there in mid-syllable. It's just like narcolepsy except her eyes don't close. The camera zooms on the figure, just starring straight ahead. Those at her sides, attempt to gently shake her awake, calling her name. Doctors on the scene say it looks like the Sleep Syndrome, the waking variety. This is the malady that has affected so many of the contestants from our show. We won't know for about a week."

Chapter Three

"Welcome back, The Runger says, Welcome back. Our fourth contestant comes to us from off world. He hails from the city of Mars Prime. His name is Remmy Manawydan. He moved back to Earth fifteen years ago when he enrolled in the University of Integrating Astral Matrix. He is the winner form the last five rounds of Dreamist. Will he go the distance? He could retire now and spend the rest of his life as a Dreamist. Will he go for the record? If he does, he has another 21 rounds to go."

His swirl begins every eye, every mind, focuses on those first few re-sequencing photons. Magic, happens as the flow of dream into matter increases. Beautiful pinks, reds, and oranges spin faster and faster. It takes a form of what appear to be two hearts, like Valentine Hearts only stacked perfectly up and down in a line. One, slightly smaller, on the top. The bottom one larger, but some how not as dense. The air is coming off it differently.

Slowly, slowly, slowly, the upper section still forming, it appears to be the head. Bulging, top heavy still spinning. There is a band around the middle of it. As it slows, eyes appear, eight eyes, looking in virtually every direction. Each eye is stationed right above a tentacle. The heart shape turns out to be the legs held together. What a hook up.

The entire being is balancing on the tips of its tentacles, just like eight little toes. How delightful, how clever and…how disturbing.

Obviously it must be called an octopus or a squid. In one coordinated, choreographed moment, he goes to his home territory. The huge creature begins by stretching its legs out straight, at an exact right angel to the body. Gently moving its weight forward, it cartwheels to its assigned place.

As this happens, the audience gets a good look at the epicenter of the tentacles. Normally, an octopus has a parrot like beak there. This time no one can be sure. There is some sort of an undergarment in place blocking the view. The octopus twirls once more, as it folds each of its eight tentacles, coiling like snakes, seating itself as though on its own throne.

This astounding, yet terrifying manifestation is met first with silence, then boos…these trail off. I starts as sympathy applause, it grows. You can hear that people admire thinking so original. Still, we have heard, a greater enthusiasm.

"The Runger says, Our fifth dreamer up is Robin Fleet. Robin is a true hermaphrodite and prefers to be addressed in the male. He is also from off world being the one hundredth person born on The Lunar Colonies. He returned to earth at age six."

The screens show an exciting array of the lunar colonies. Robin's Childhood pictures, his other siblings, Mom, Dad and the whole family. A snapshot of him appears, in cockpit of the 1921 Bi-Plane he rebuilt. He smiles as the proud pilot. Next are pictures of him graduating the Deep Space Academy as an Ensign.

Currently, he is awaiting assignment as ships counselor on the first ship to go beyond Sirius. He will also be logging information on the effect of long space flight, as well as about dreaming out of our solar system. He has just turned 33 years of age.

"The Runger says, Robin, manifest your dream body."

As it begins, it looks like sparkling confetti has been dropped into a whirlwind. What is unusual about it is that there are right angles forming with in it, each traced by an individual confetti. One appearing right after another. More and more appear. It looks as though some structure is being created. As more mass is slipping into the stream, the angles expand forming new relationships with each other.

It's shades of gray, black, perhaps some very dark reds and browns swirl by. As the slowing occurs, the final angles unfold and viola, a house. A domicile, from the 1800's it is Victorian, clearly. Its last rotations landed it exactly where it is supposed to be in order for the games to start.

"Wait, wait, says the Runger, this place, it's one of the frat houses from Integrating Astral Matrix University! Oh, which one is it?"

Quite as though, the building could hear, three triangles appear on a plaque above the door. It's the Theta, Theta, Theta frat house.

"This structure was demolished seven years ago to build The Franklin Building, a new dormitory on campus. The Runger declares, how interesting. Haunted extremely, do you think? Nothing like frat ghosts to scare ya, eh? What do they say, 'Boo, we've run out of beer?'"

The audience breaks into laughter and applause. This evolves into cat calls and animal sounds, similar to what one might hear at any frat party or college football rally. Go Theta! is actually chanted.

For a moment, the house seems to catch and hold this vibe. One could imagine such a party going on inside the house, but when the audience dies down the house becomes stark, dark again, all but lifeless. The contrast is bone chilling. Three of tonight's contestants have slept in that new dorm. Two others happen to have been members of Theta, Theta, Theta.

"Our sixth and final contestant is from right here on Earth, in fact New Pittsburgh, on the island of Midway. The Runger says, her name is Jony Quixon and she is also a true hermaphrodite. She graduated from Integrating Astral Matrix University almost ten years ago. She is working as a dreams manager, for Terraform, a company creating a land bridge, between Midway Island and Tahiti."

Once again the announcer places our attention on the giant video panels. Beautiful pictures of tropical islands, followed by, close-ups of Jony's life, friends, where she works. Orbital pictures of the Land Bridge, projections of the finished project, all saunter by. Completed, it makes a perfect triangle a slightly different blue from the rest of the waters.

"It's like an identification, a tribal marking, a tattoo, a signature of the beings that inhabit this world. What a wonderful blessing man can be for the planet.

Three years from now, they will be building a similar bridge from Hawaii to Tahiti, thus creating the reality of a triangular sub-ocean in the pacific. This man made ocean is going to be used by the World Life Commission and it will feed us all.

OK, Jony Quixon, The Runger says, its time to suit up, show us what ya got."

On cue, the holographic god of wind begins to spin yet

another dream body. The glistening luminal particles begin. This time they are a dark aquamarine blue. Slipping down the very center of the column of charged particles. It makes this beautiful blue shaft. The tone of the holo-wind changes and bright purple flash causes a shift. Suddenly, the shaft is surrounded by a purple sphere. The sphere begins to fill with a lighter pink matter. After spinning a few more moments, all of the contents just fall into a man. The sphere itself comes to a stop.

All eyes study the face of this man. Puzzlement, confusions, the audience does not know what to do, with this. The figure is short and wide, the fingers are thick and blunt, the eyebrows sit on a bony ridge. The brain case barely exceeds brow in height. He is a Neandertal.

"The Runger thinks somebody got in touch with their unconscious. Maybe just a little too seriously. This is one of the third year dreaming school assignments. No. No, they're giving me an all clear from the hermaphrodite's IG. The Chief Dream Coach has given it the go ahead."

Again all eyes return to the Neanderthal, still in his beautiful blue sphere. He makes eye contact back. The thing is he...is no longer Neandertal. He has gained several inches of height. He is standing more erect. The Club he had been holding has disappeared. He is now holding a spear.

He has become Cro-Magnon. The clothing is still animal

skins, however, he now wears some sort of medicine bag or talisman around the neck. As the man slowly continues to spin, he continues to evolve. Another rotation brings him up to Homo Sapien. The animal skin clothing, is now cloth, however coarse. A bow and arrow replace the spear and the talisman is now metallic, probably bronze.

The next spin brings him into one of the teen centuries. Perhaps the sixteenth century judging by the frilly clothes, and the pomp in his hair. The adornment around the throat has become a golden cross. The archery set has become a musket/rifle in his hand.

Once more he turns and clearly becomes a citizen of the twentieth century. The clothing is a dark blue pinstripe suit. A tie and tie clasp have replaced the cross. He is wearing chromed aviator sunglasses. By now he is standing perhaps six three. The weapon has been replaced with a briefcase.

The next rotation brings him into the current century. There is no question the clothing is hot! The fabrics represent the triumph of man against laundry. The shoes are the latest in sneaker meets technology. They are adorned with fins, lights and data sensors. They contain a generator that charges a battery with every step taken. The medallion is a multiphaseic shield emitter with color field projection gear. The briefcase has been replaced with the latest wristband technology, with the sunglasses having transmuted into the Vi-fos.

Shall we say, the crowd explodes with applause. It would have gone for fifteen minutes. However he begins to spin again. A quarter million people gasp simultaneously. Clearly the audience had expected him to stop. As the transmutation begins the auditorium is perfectly silent.

The next spin makes him taller, well above seven feet. His body becomes elegantly elongated. The clothing takes on a uniform-like character. All one color, like a suit, but more along the lines of a flight suit. It has no visible pockets or bulges. Triple chevrons adorn his shoulders. There is an unknown insignia located at the center of the heart. The glasses remain, still mirrored and simply adhere to the face as though they are part of him. Apparently nothing is held in his hands.

His new form, is being greeted by absolute silence. After a moment the rotation again starts, and again, the sound of a quarter million people gasping. The audience is mirroring our curiosity, and fear, about what man will become.

As the process comes to a halt, the man is taller still. He now has more of a hermaphroditic figure. The suit has been replaced with a skintight fabric a green gold in color. No Medallion, no glasses, and nothing hand held.

The crowd searches every detail of his person. A purple cloud begins to fill his beautiful sphere. It fills from the bottom up. The sphere begins to rotate again, continuing for several minutes. Occasionally, it would slow and then emit a light pulse.

This occurs seven consecutive times, the light pulses coinciding with a rainbow. First the red flash, then the orange, yellow etcetera.

The sphere's rotation builds up slowly. It's spinning faster than ever before. With no warning what so ever. it shatters. Little pieces of it go in every direction. The cloud of purple smoke that had been inside of it remains in place. It stands in the form of the sphere, just in mid-air, perfectly for a moment and then slowly descends toward the stage, revealing…

The appearance is now more alien than human. Standing over nine feet tall, he has the presence of some kind of a lord. The eyes, perfectly visible, are huge in comparison to an average adult. The iris of each eye is probably an inch in diameter, colored in a stunning purple, with bright blue fibers. Hairless, the skull is enlarged, perhaps a third, to half again, the size of the normal human brain casing. No one can tell if this being is wearing clothes or it is just skin. No note of navel, nipples or genitalia just seamless…

Silence, the audience sits as though in trance. Not a word, not a sound, he raises his hands in the air. It's a sign of triumph, like when a boxer raises his hands after a victory. Slowly, he turns and struts, to his place in his home petal. It's as though watching some wrestler doing a peacock walk to receive his prize.

Still silence until the host, breaks the spell by starting to talk. "Wow ladies and gentlemen, what a contest we are having this evening. What an unusual assortment of dreaming bodies! The Runger says, two men two women and two hermaphrodites, balanced indeed. This show may go down in history as one of the turning points in dreaming evolution. Wait, wait, The Runger, has just been given this news bulletin."

The 4DV panels again light up, with pictures of 2084's Dreamist, Red Jaguar. He successfully held the title for 13 consecutive battles. In those days, it's an unheard of record. He became the most widely publicized man on the planet, for more than a year. His name is synonymous with the charismatic appeal, which is being a Dreamist. His history has been exemplary. He regularly addresses, the planetary congress on brilliant new ideas, for the future betterment of our society.

"Ladies and Gentlemen: The Runger is mortified to announce that Red Jaguar has been found in a comatose state!! He was last seen in public three days ago. Doctors have identified his condition as a post-event trauma. He has joined the ranks of those who appear on this show and end up with the sleep disorder known as Continuous Sleep Syndrome."

The first case of perpetual sleep disorder began on the July Fourteenth, 2061 show. A contestant had been in a battle with someone projecting a tetrahedron, a three-sided pyramid. Right before it ended, the tetrahedron peeled one of its sides from the bottom up. The player was taken by surprise. He became rolled up inside the sheet of tetrahedron. It was like some gigantic one celled animal had sacrificed a layer of skin to insure the safety of the whole organism. The point at the tip of the triangle looped up and pinned him down even more. The tetrahedron then gave off a sound. The tone had the effect of shattering the sheet. The player's dream body, all rolled up inside, shattered as well.

It was the person projecting the tetrahedron that had won, as the last one asleep. Shattering his dreaming body, along with the piece of tetrahedron, woke up the other player just like that.

The tetrahedron jammed in the machinery. No one could wake the guy up. No one could get the pyramid to drop photonic cohesion. After three days of theory, investigation and debate the entire studio was rebooted. Which of course took an additional day.

That additional day was also the first official announcement that the contestant had been disqualified for the Continuous Sleep Syndrome. Since then, he has been asleep for almost thirty-six years.

"Let's get back to tonight's show. The Runger says, Let the games begin! A cry as old as Rome. Let the Games Begin!" The pulse from these words goes through the entire Dream Dome audience, throughout the entire planet, off planet to Mars and our other colonies. The six contestants, each at a pose, standing boldly, neatly, each on their own home territory, all come to attention.

Chapter Four

I look around at the other players. Each one is confident that they will be able to command the dream. With the crowd chanting, the pressure is building. I see the octopus creeping his tentacles up behind the insectoid. What is this urge that drives us? Still man must compete. The octopus is silent, advancing. He starts gaining significant territory.

The grasshopper is caught off guard. The tentacle penetrates the auric field at a weak spot in the back of the heart chakra. This weakens the bug. Tentacle after tentacle wrap around the insectoid. The grasshopper can do little to inflict damage on her captor.

The two struggle. In a sudden and totally unexpected move; the octopus unwound his tentacles so fast that it threw the bug straight into the open door of the frat house. It's just like a fastball pitch. There is the sound of the impact against one of the interior walls. The audience and the other players laugh and laugh.

The insect doesn't reappear. The house remains dark. There is the sound of a door slamming. A few moments later a second door slams. A third, a fourth, then more and more are heard. There are so many doors slamming it makes a sound like some horrible machine. It is monstrous, entraining fear into the rhythm of the hearts of the audience.

It ends abruptly. There is a loud, well, crunch. We all know the sound, it's the sound of a big bug getting stepped on. Or in this case, slammed in a door. The audience in a single voice says, yuck. You can tell the show is going good. About four thousand people throughout the house, actually throw up. Who knows how many in the entire audience?

Still, the frat house remains dark and silent. Quietly at first, a steady stream of little ha-ha-has, trailing out of it, like a little twist of smoke, coming out of the chimney.

"Its official, The Runger says, the dreamer has awoken. Stella Orion, is out of the game. She said, she somehow lost faith, trapped in the frat house. It's like a maze in there. She felt she could not possibly get home, to her own territory, to then re-initialize her next dreaming body. The Runger says, how odd, well see about this house."

The attention instantly switches to me, Kabel Newstarr,

the General from the dreaming wars. The Future-Human and I have become involved in a primordial-wrestling match. I'm surprised by what strength he has in those elongated arms. I easily lift him above my head, with my huge bear arms. I toss him good, but he lands like a ballerina. The crowd, to say the least, is amused.

Again he approaches me, how can he dare to compete with me in brawn? I decide to stop toying with him and crush him when, out of nowhere, splash. We're suddenly engulfed in water. This must be that water being, what astoundment.

Future-Human slips away when my attention is distracted by the surprise bath. I can see through the clear water. My cubs are rallying, they are clawing at the skin of the drop. How thick can this stuff possibly be? I thought my claws would go right through it. No, the skin seems capable of being stretched, but won't break. The cubs are looking at me from the other side. Ya know, it just occurred to me, I haven't been breathing lately.

Just as I think this, I see a tentacle go through the skin and raps around one of the cubs. How did octopus get in here? The cub didn't see it coming. She's hauled into the wash with the rest of us. The octopus sends his arms toward Future-Human. Next, those tentacles begin moving toward me, everything goes dark, absolute black, no input. Is my dreaming body dead? No? I can still sense my form. Did the octopus set off the ink? If I can't see, how will I know what to do?

Panic, abject panic, sets off a fail-safe in my mind. My basic commando training kicks in. There is always a door in any dream. How many times do I have to hear the sergeant, say it? Where is it this time? Where is the door this time? I look inwardly, for the exit. Don't look decide. Decide where the door lies, decide where it's. Corporal, decide where the door is, this instant.

It's coming into focus. There is movement. I see my claws strain against the fabric of the surface of the water. I realize that I'd asked, "How difficult could breaking the skin be?" What a negative command to give. Sloppy thinking for a dream... I'll never win like this. The failsafe goes off again. "Never win," Who is writing this? I claim my dreaming power.

The colors around me change. My dreaming enters balance, even harmony... I have it, command of my dream. I'm commanding the dream door to re-appear.

I begin dreaming that the Future-Human is folding, him self up into a fetal pose. Tensing every muscle, he charges himself to give off an electronetic pulse. A lightning bolt generates, deep with in him. I give the sound. The sound is the activator code, for the lightning bolt. The bear larynx reproduces it perfectly. Those purple eyes roll up as the lightning flash comes out the top of his head and the bottom of his feet. A perfect arc!

The water explodes into billions of drops. As each drop leaves the field parameters of the waveform generators, it stops existing. The first three concentric rings of audience seating, roughly ninety thousand people, would have been soaked. What happens, when that many pieces of resequencing matter drop cohesion, is that there is a visual phenomenon. It resembles those little plasma beings, the purple lightning that lives in a little glass ball, children used to keep them as pets. Something like arcing electricity, but all vanishing a few feet from the first row.

The cubs and I are sent flying. Future-Human lands in the circle directly opposite me. The pulse that was given off leaves me a little groggy. I look around and see one of the cubs, she looks like she has drowned. This thought alone, is good enough to initiate cascade failure in that cub. The cub drops photonic cohesion, with what feels like some of my internal organs. Command, command, I place my attention on my dreaming center.

I see the Frat House with stood the storm, still down spouts flooding, eves dripping. What a strategy this dreamer has. How truly female. Just to wait, it all must come to you.

Suddenly I feel curious about the house. What has happened to the bug? Was that crunch as gruesome as it sounded? As though hypnotized, I begin to steer this enormous bear body, toward the entrance. The octopus, in what I later consider to have been an act of kindness, literally trips me with his tentacles.

I realize my huge bear body has fallen. Face down on the stage I see the feet of Future-Human approach. The octopus makes short work of holding my front legs. As I struggle to regain my posture, Old Futureoid, produces a small purple crystal sphere. As I watch helpless, a light appears in the center of the ball. As I look at it, I begin to lose focus. It becomes way too bright, way too fast.

Suddenly, I'm back in the dreaming wars. I'm a commander. I'm co-dreaming with 259 other dream soldiers. I remember the mission. I remember every person in our team. The entire group of us is set up. Intelligence has been telling us that the enemy is hidden, lying flat, in a cemetery. Their strategy is to use this tactic to surprise us. When we arrive at the graveyard, a new energy weapon goes off. As I look around it's mostly us lying there. We are tricked into dreaming our own deaths. What a night mirror. This is why there are never any accurate statistics given on dreaming troop casualties.

I must maintain dream consciousness. I know that the pulse from the purple ball coincided, with the zap from the energy weapon in the flash back. I have to regain command of the dream. Well, more like I choose to be in command of the dream. I'm not in a cemetery, I'm in the future. I'm a contestant on the Dreamist show. I'm holding my own. I'm inside of some kind of big, big body.

I begin to sense the big bear body again. It's like I've come back into her from the air above her. All my consciousness drains from the body of the behemoth bear. Rushing out as though I'm a dam, bursting. It's all going into the cub. I'm going into the cub.

The mother bear body has begun to initiate cascade failure. Am I all the way in the cub body? Inside my IG, I hear one of the engineers say, two thousand teraquads weren't sent. Weren't sent? Am I all here?

The engineer says, I'm on it, boss. It's just stuff about the energy index ratio between running the big body and the little one. It's nothing essential. We may have one strong little cub there.

All eyes are on the cub. I'm seeing out of the cub's eyes. I feel fine. The body is very responsive. This is about the only difference I notice. The octopus is stung badly, almost dead. He has a tentacle, almost touching his home territory. In order to help this one, I have to leave my own territory.

Future-Human starts to drag the octopus toward the rim of the stage. If a dream body leaves the stage it will loose cohesion, automatically. If this happens, the waker of the octopus, will wake up and be out.

Octopus, octopus, get back in your dream body. Octopus, come on. Wait, what am I doing? It's OK, if I let the octopus take responsibility for its own beingness. I must take care of myself first. Then I can help. Ah, breaking the "hope" habit. I loose every time, I stop watching my own helm.

As I watch life starts to come back into the overgrown

mollusk. He attaches several tentacles to the stage. Future-Human is pulling them up one sticker at a time. The octopus gets a couple of arms around Future-Human. The struggle becomes the center of attention through out the audience. The rest of the players and I stop and watch, just like the audience.

Future-Human stands on his own two legs, thus regaining some advantage. There wasn't much the octopus could do about it, because he has his tentacles full, dealing with the struggle. The octopus wraps around the entire upper body of his opponent. Blue-purple eyes aren't much good if you're blind folded. Future-Human and the octopus go over the side of the stage. Everything gasps simultaneously.

Just as the weight is shifting, and the duo begins to fall, the Future-Human manages to get a hand free. As they go over, the edge of the stage is caught. The palm of the hand acts like a suction cup. Every bit of both dream bodies looses cohesion, at the same moment. All except the hand, it's like a severed body part laying, still pulsing, just on the edge of the stage.

All that remains of the two is the hand of Future-Human. Almost immediately there is a spotlight on the hand. It lays there, seemingly devoid of life. But wait, the sixth finger is moving, it's pushing the hand up. A few last signals leaking through the wires? Post traumatic event syndrome?

The hand reanimates. Just like all those children's stories about the Adam's Family. The hand comes to its "fingers." It's just like a little figure. Standing up right it begins to "walk." Slowly at first. The audience breaks up! As the hand becomes more sophisticated, it trots around the stage, to peals of laughter. It's heading to its home territory where it can regenerate.

I decide to do something about this. As I start toward the hand, the water, which has been all over everything, causes my cub body to slide, dangerously close to the edge of the stage.

Again, the audience laughs hysterically. I'm upside down and sliding. My first thought is to get traction. My bear joints don't move the same way I'm used to, but I do manage to stop myself from going over.

Back on all fours I start toward the hand. This reaction is virtually instinct, generated by the bear body. I'm sort of watching it happen. Missing information? Maybe it would be a better idea to head to my home petal and transmute a new dream body, while I still can…

The water, water, everywhere…is starting to "quake." I've never seen water do this before. Its as though specialized parts of it rise up and fill in a greater depth. At first it seems to be at random. It is definitely forming something… Now there is an over all geometric form. It's so familiar.

The mass began to collect itself, exactly in the dead center of the stage. Since the water covered the giant drop's original territory this was acceptable. The first part of the form that I recognized, the first part of it that came into focus, was a tooth.

A human tooth, it's set on a jawbone. More teeth are forming. As I look up it appears to be forming as a gigantic human skull. As it's vibrational rate speeds up just slightly faster, it became crystal, transparent. Now, it is a fully formed crystal skull and it's optically clear.

I stare in disbelief, poor dreamsmanship I admit. Disbelief is the first weakness in dreaming. Nonetheless, I am impressed. Yet, the frat house… When the skull manifested itself in the center, it took up a little territory from each of the six sections. The house, the frat house, was half inside the skull. The skull, just formed itself, in the same space and same time as the house.

You could see Theta, Theta, Theta, from any part of the skull you look. If you look in both eyes you see the house. Actually the way it's situated, the house is occupying the lower back of the skull. It crosses my mind that that old house was actually in the position of the subconscious of the skull. Yuck, what a horrid subconscious to have. Not for me thanks.

The house itself didn't seem all too happy about this turn of events. The hand and I walk around to get a closer look at the house. The fail-safe I installed about "the house hypnotizing me" activates, quite loudly, I must say. Still, hand and I can see or feel what pain it seems to be in. By some mysterious process, it's obvious that the house is no longer a threat.

The entire structure gives off an audible sound, as though the front door has become a mouth. The boards, of the doorframe, begin to spontaneously splinter. They make a horrible sound as they snap. When the first board crunches, it seems like I actually hear the sound of the grasshopper, commingling with the sound of the boards.

The house is shattering right in front of me. Every board is splintering again and again. The entire structure has some how taken on this code. Each smaller splinter, itself splinters. Within moments the house reduces itself to sawdust, just falling out of the side of the skull. The entire stage is now covered with a fine layer of this dust.

Both hand and I head for our home petals. My opponent makes it there first. I watch as a small cloud of dust swirls up. This is necessary in order to get a clean connection to the equipment. There must be a good contact made in order to regenerate.

The spiral of energy begins. The transmutation sequences in, meanwhile I just make it to my home territory, as we all hear…

"The Runger says, it's the time of break. Our beloved octopus, projected by Remmy Manawydan is officially awake."

The focus goes to Remmy. He is sweaty, puffy the way we are when were awoken out of a deep sleep abruptly. His head coach is standing next to him.

"Remmy, tell The Runger your ok."

The coach speaks, saying that he is a little shaken up but has a clean bill of health. Being just suddenly dropped out of cohesion like that can really disorient the dreamer. But he's gonna be OK.

"This makes The Runger feel good. Well see ya in the post game show. Here we go, now forward to the games."

Chapter Five

I'm watching the swirl being created by what was the hand, it's very similar to the one, Jony Quixon created before. I wonder if it will be a duplicate of Future-man. The same shaft of blue light, I recognize it. Maybe it's just an element of style, in this individual's dreaming.

It's the same energy signature as before. The shaft reaches critical mass and pulses, this time, into an unbelievable blue green sphere. The sight of this causes my heart to change rhythm for a moment. As the mass slows its rotation, everyone, including me, is focusing on the clouds of matter within the sphere.

Moments go by. Every one wonders what will be inside the sphere when it finishes. An exact number of rotations, per second is reached, it's beginning to stabilize. The moments go by, everyone is holding their breath. The swirling mass just drops. It drops into nothing. Or so it seems, it's still a sphere. The sphere yes, but in another dimension? The ball becomes animated, it moves up and down in the air. You can recognize it begin to spin, even in its dream of spinning. Faster and faster it goes.

As the rpm increases, it condenses its mass, smaller and smaller, denser and denser, until it becomes an orb, about one foot in diameter. As it does this, the color is also condensing. The color is more than saturated. It has become such a dark blue green, as to fool the eye. You know how royal blue can be mistaken for black? It floats there. The audience applauds, just a few at first, a sprinkling here and there. For the majority, the trance is still too deep.

An odd thing is happening. I see a little swirl of house dust go up. The frat house must be reinitializing a dream body. Spontaneously, it's just happening. It's just like a little tornado. It's about ten inches tall when a second one starts. Almost immediately, the entire stage is transformed into little storms everywhere like some odd little storm front, an arbitrary, somehow bizarrely stylized weather condition.

I find out that, there is a cellular level memory, built into my bear dreaming body. All bears have it, in fact all animals have a built in sensitivity to weather systems especially the tornado. The body I'm in has become sluggish. All of the little cyclones have begun to join into one big tall tornado. Deep with in the bear there is primordial fear. Primordial fear, how's this, for an echo back? The bear originally greeted the crowd with a deep roar, designed to frighten. Terror out, terror back, its one of those natural harmonics.

The wind is going faster and faster. It's about as tall as my body standing at its full height. I claw at it repeatedly. The tornado is actually chasing me. I'm fighting the wind, harder and harder. The more I resist the harder it shoves. I'm loosing command of the dream. In the moment, of the fear, of this thought, I feel my four feet loosing contact with the stage. I'm being swept up like a leaf in an autumn breeze. The cub dreaming body is hoisted up and flown all the way around the stage many times.

Inside my IG they know I'm loosing command of the dream. I'm suddenly a child again. I remember the teacher asking if any one has ever had a night mirror. Every one in class, took a turn telling their electrifying experiences with super natural dragons, etc. Yes, everybody but *moi*. They all look at...me. I never had a night-mirror, at least none I recall. I'm about age nine. I'm a normal girl in so many ways. I remember looking at my eyes in the mirror. I have unusually large irises was my thought.

One night mom brings home a movie that is a little more than she expects. She knows that I like movies about animals, especially monkeys. It's the original version. It's cool. It's called "King Kong."

About half way through my mother suddenly let out a sincere

scream. Every alert I own goes off. This night, I take the vow that every child takes, the one that they will protect and defend their mother at any cost. And so it is spoken.

In late night, as I come into my mother's dream. Her dream-scape is identical to the movie. I can see my mother already held helpless, already held in his mighty, sweaty, hairy, hand. Ma, I never realized how much you look like Fay Ray.

In my dream, I pull myself to my full child height, approximately one-yard. I face the monster monkey and I say, "Put the babe down mister. You are so unauthorized." And the monkey just knew it. He bought it. Next day, mom told me she would never watch any movie from the last century, period.

Back on stage, the tornado has begun to shrink, drawing its mass into its new form. The cub is dropped from this autumn breeze with a bone crunching impact. I remember where I lost command. The sight of the edge of the stage coming at me set it off.

Back when I was on all fours, I started toward the hand with six fingers. The reaction was from the bear body, not from me. I remember thinking, maybe it would be a better idea to head to my home petal and transmute a new dream body, while I still can…

The dream command code, "while I still can?" How could I have missed it? How could I have given up my power so easily? I've been dreaming someone else's dream ever since.

The cyclone of dust, reaching critical mass, drops into existence. Whirling more slowly the color of yellow and green formed a huge, beautifully coiling tropical snake. A python, there's just no question about it. Must be a fifty footer or more.

While the audience watches this, my little cub body is landing, exactly in the center of my home petal. What a shot! It's like the best day ever, on Wheel of Fortune. I'd better get into a new dream body quick. The code! The fail-safe goes off. I must find my dreaming center. But, before I can accomplish this, my focus returns to the game. Seeing the faces of my opponents, frightens me again, it throws me even more off balance. I slip...

I'm back in school I'm about twenty-one. The teacher is asking the class if any one can remember their first night mirror? I'm the only one who said I didn't. My dreams are always the good times going on. That was exactly what I thought as a child. *"Laissez le bon temps rouler, oui."* My uncle Kane and aunt Abelline, are from the south of France and spoke the language to me, as a child. I am named after them, Kabel.

My team, in the IG, know that someone will attack the cub body, unless I can get a new dream body manifesting and quickly. The coach and I have worked out a strategy of stand by dream bodies. The team picks a colony of bees, for the best possible adaptability to the circumstances of the game. It's loading...It's a go.

The cub disappears as the holoswhurl begins. The audience,

the skull, the sphere, the snake, all look at me. I can feel the drain the machinery puts on my mind, I'm being sucked through. Here we go, I don't fight it any more, I am pulled into the rotation. I can feel something forming. I'm at mass. Hurry, hurry, here comes the drop… What am I becoming? I am still spinning too fast.

I start to stabilize, as the rotation comes to a stop, sitting here, in a divine happiness is my inner child. My twenty-one year old body, loaded in the projector. I must have given a command, while experiencing, being my college freshman self. I sit here slightly dizzy, collecting my systems, and well, lets just say scantily clad. Well,OK, naked. It's really a good thing that I am this good looking.

I see the three of them staring at me, the sake , the skull and the sphere. They're are so in shock. They are forgetting where they are. What they are doing…? Why are they just standing there? Because I'm naked? No! It's because I'm naked and this gorgeous, Oh-Ya!!

I look back at them and repeat what my uncle told me so many nights, just before I fell asleep, *"Prendre votre coupe chaude. Laissez le bon temps rouler, oui."* Take your hot shot! Let the good times roll! I place my attention on the aquamarine sphere, it's the first to move.

It levitates and begins to float towards me, but at the last minute, it goes to the skull, totally by surprise. It enters the crystal structure as though by magic. It simply, gracefully, flows around inside of it, as though it, were again somehow filled with water.

It enters from the side. Inside, like a bubble in soda, the sphere floats up to where the third eye would be. Obviously this has an adverse effect. A titanic struggle begins. The skull quakes, expands, contracts. The movements mimic breathing, but a labored breathing, for sure. The color begins to change. It's becoming a lighter green. As though the sphere itself, were leaking some green pigmentation into its crystalline depths. The overall color is getting darker and darker green.

Without warning, from inside the skull, the sphere pulses to a diameter much wider than the skull itself. The sphere, just stays pulsed out. The sphere has engulfed its opponent. It's a total capture.

The sphere slowly contracts its mass becoming denser and denser. This process is accompanied by a sound like a snowball being formed. Finally it's only about eight inches in diameter. Clearly everyone could see the skull held inside the sphere. In a prison, a captive, held frozen, like some surreal piece of taxidermy.

Everyone is about to look at me! I can feel it coming. No, no it's MY dream. I dream the snake is stung by the crystal ball. The sphere immediately begins to taunt the snake. The skull, all the while is peering out from the blue green interior.

The sphere and the snake go eye to eye. Zap, it's the same pulse that left the bear groggy. This time it hit the snake. Its body convulsing while it instinctively snaps at the air in front of the ball. The powerful jaws are missing again and again.

The python retreats by curling itself up. The arcing current has run out. Gathering its strength, silently it looks at the floating orb. We are all looking at the ball wondering what's next? The reason I had the ball sting the snake originally, was to get the snake to attack the ball.

The snake, lunging ten feet in the air, snaps that sphere right down his throat, just like that. The Python, quickly moving the ball, deep with in its long, long body. The snake stands up on its coil. The move is totally smooth, just like catching a football. The audience goes wild. The reptile begins to do a victory undulation, when...

The dreamer of the crystal skull suddenly awakens. Later, Mendel, will tell the post show interviewer that it was like being buried alive twice, at the same time. "The claustrophobia overwhelmed me. I retreated to the waking body, as an instinctive self-defense. I know, I know, this is exactly what this show is about, not doing."

The shock of feeling the skull die, within the dream body of the sphere causes, the sphere's creator, to come back with us as well. Jony, will tell the officials, that when Mandell awoke from his skull dream, that she became caught in a current, a thought form, that may have been from, an illegal enhancement. Serious charges!

One of the great reforms brought by the dreaming wars, is what we refer to as the Dreaming Laws. It got so bad that companies begin hiring teams of dreamers to influence sales. Well at least at first it was sales, then votes, it just continued to escalate. Now it's felonious to use a crystal or any external enhancement, to willfully influence someone's dreams.

Everyone is very sensitive about this sort of manipulation. As an experienced dreamer, Jony felt what may be a mechanical boost, in the thought stream that conducts the trip, from sleeper to being awake.

Chapter Six

The snake places his attention on me. Our eyes meet. I stair into that cold reptilian look the tongue bolting, the skin glistening. I think to myself, OK come and get me. The snake begins to move its tail around behind me, as though I'm not supposed to notice.

Still, stare to stare, I am hypnotizing the snake. Clearly, I am dreaming the snake. I am the snake. I am the snake's thoughts. The snake begins to wrap its body around me. Tighter, it wraps around my legs. I can feel my legs from the snake's body, the snake's brain. Then the head rises in the air. Well above me, looking down at me. Still eye contact remains un-broken.

Suddenly it lunges, its mouth opening, as it comes at me. I disappear, swallowed into the snake. My legs kick back and forth, as the snake again rises to his height. The audience must be getting quite a show. I'm, I'm just advertising, all over town. Well, maybe I'll get a date out of all this.

I'm actually pulling myself down throat of the reptile. As I'm doing this, I am dreaming that I'm waking up. This command goes into the system. I feel it. I watch it course through the wires. I've always been able to dream anything I can think of. Dreaming that you are awake is the oldest trick in the book.

The crowd boos, the crowd cheers. Thousands and thousands of people all booing. They throw things at the snake. The thousands cheering start to jeer the ones booing. Fights can break out, but generally the fans keep it down. There are some serious crowd control mechanisms, built into the dome, and everybody knows it.

Moments later the IG from Robin's team burst open... She's awake. Her team is exiting. Python Rules! Python Rules. Fans, behind the young hermaphrodite, have made signs. The camera is eating it up.

"Here comes The Runger, The Runger says congratulations Robin! It is my honor to bestow you the title of..." The announcer puts his hand on his ear. "No wait, wait, I'm hearing from General Newstarr's IG.. She is still in slumber. She is the winner. Stand by...Yes it's official. Newstarr is the next Dreamist."

In my IG, My coach, is saying come on, back here with us. I start telling him I'm dreaming that I'm tickling a giant snake and it wakes up and becomes a robin… The coach is checking my irises. He is smiling from ear to ear. The rest of the team is making sure I'm OK.

Groggy, but I'm here. I feel the air from outside flood the IG. It's cool. It's wonderful. The sound of the crowd is unexpected. These things are completely sound proof. You'd never know there are that many people out there. A delight goes through me, like you get if you leave a warm tub and go into a cold part of the house. I Love it. We step through the door. The host, the crowd, all here, the level of excitement is let's just say, whelming.

"The Runger says, Complete Feng! Wow, Kabel, do you know how to come form behind? Oh-Ya, tell us how you did it."

"I took command of the final dream, after remembering the false dream code, I put in. I claimed my dreaming power and began to dream, the snake eating me. As I am being swallowed, I dream that I'm waking up. The big lug fell for it. Robin didn't realize the loss of command. I believe there may have been a sway, from the instincts of the snake body. As a natural predator, the body itself, goes for the kill, directly I mean.

But I gotta say, My Runger! This program puts military dreaming in an entirely different place in my mind. This is one of the fondest, most exciting things I've ever had the honor of doing."

"Congratulations, The Runger says, congratulations! General Newstarr, you are conferred officially, the rank of Dreamist. Great job, Kabel! It ends like a fairy tale, says The Runger."

I open my mouth and out comes, "To dream a dream is to open a box. What ever comes out is another piece of the puzzle. You are the puzzle. Once you get enough of the pieces you'll realize, they are really all just one piece, in different forms. Once all the pieces become interchangeable, you can walk between the worlds."

Thirteen days later, it's announced that Jony, the hermaphrodite who claims that an illegal crystal, has been used to awaken her, during the show, is pronounced as having waking sickness. The contestants that get this are OK for a few days, but then they just sit and stare. Caretakers have to spray a mist into their eyes, so that the surface of the lens does not damage from dehydration. Jony has already been institutionalized with it.

Chapter Seven

After the show, my sleeping patterns changes, shall we say dramatically. Let us say that, I simply did not sleep. At first, it's the natural exuberance. Actually having won the title of a Dreamist, what a kick. I just pack every moment with excitement.

The guys from the IG, are pretty close, I've known some of them since the Dreaming Wars. They've been calling. They tell me that thirteen days, without so much as a nap, is unusual. I feel perfectly great. Finally, I go down to have it checked out.

Having seen the wards of "casualties" from my dream troops, I really can't take the show or its potential dangers as much of a threat. Still, I'm glad to have it checked out.

The doctors tell me that this is not too unusual a reaction to the "stress" that has somehow managed to attach itself, to me.

For a time, I feel that I may be one of the people who, never sleep again. It couldn't be, I seem perfectly normal to everyone, including myself. There are simply none of the accompanying mental problems. I shrug my shoulders, and go on with my revitalizing life

In the next thirteen days, after my ok from the dream doctors, I am on exactly one dozen talk shows. A particular house of fashion, desires that I, associate my name, with their line. They would do the "Python" look, from the show. My life, it's like reaching thrust, to achieve orbit. I must say, simply WOW, in every direction.

The weeks blend into months, well I'm getting a lot done. I clean and organize and then, I clean and organize and for a break, I would do some cleaning and, ah…organizing. My life is becoming very focused. Everything about me accelerates. I begin to read the latest works in advanced mathematics and to my astoundment, I understand them. It's like I'm growing brain. It all seems easier and easier.

Then one day I finish the dishes, sit down on the couch and fall asleep for a hundred and eighty seven thousand, two hundred minutes. Exactly. That's 90 days. I take a nap for three months.

After such an extended nap, one would be expected to return to consciousness slowly. Me, nothing like it, I open my eyes and am fully aware of my conscious self. It seems like I have only been asleep ten minutes. It's as though I just stepped through some kind of a door. Bang, I'm here in my living room. Yet, I must admit, I am disoriented.

There is something else unusual about the way I awaken. Ya know how you can be dreaming about grasping something? So much so, that every muscle in the hand is tense. Then when you wake up, you look down, and viola, there it is, but just for a second, and then it disappears. The palm of your hand comes into focus as it vanishes.

This time, it vanishes not. Not even a little. It's unnerving. In my hand is a book of matches. Clutched, held on too as though for dear life. The matches are from a night club, called The Dreamy Time Club. Inside the cover, a phone number and a man's name written in green ink.

Chapter Eight

There is yet, something else odd about the way in which I wake up. I wake up and it's exactly ninety days after the date of the show. I check it on a calendar. How can this be? I cannot have just slept for ninety days and during the same ninety days lived the Dreamist life and been on all those talk shows.

I utter the word 4Dv! My wall comes to life, a prize from the show. As the picture comes up, I could see my own face on the previews for tonight's show. My, I do look nuclear hot. Wait a minute that show has already been filmed. How does this work? Well this is gonna be interesting. I'm sitting here now and I'm going to be on Globe Grid in an hour. Maybe, I can call in and talk to myself on the air.

On this particular show, there is going to be a second

Dreamist, the guy that writes those mystery novels. Maybe I can tell him about my last three months and he can solve the mystery.

How is it possible that I've been asleep ninety days and I have also been living a waker life? I must have been dreaming right here on my couch, when I was being examined by he dreaming commission doctors. They have reports, readings of various body functions and active recordings of synaptic brain maps. Ya, but of what? How does this work? This is getting more interesting. Or is it confusing? I'm going with interesting.

I know I just slept for 90 days. The automatic dream journal goes on when ever I fall asleep. It logged 2160 hours straight, but without a single entry. Yet, I can account for being in the waking world, with absolute scientific proof, that I have been up and around for the last three months. Except, I don't really have a memory of the time, exactly. Its like I'm forgetting my life, just like forgetting dreams. What few memories I do have, disappear the moment I place my attention on them. Gone like a drop in an ocean. I don't get it. There is no way…

Another mystery is whose number is this. Is his name really Alouenne? Who is named Alouenne? I'm just going to call him and find out if he has any answers.

When it connects, a voice answers, saying Hello, Dreamy Time Club… I thought this would be this guy's private line. Once again I am amazed, what is the Dreamy Time Club?

"Hello, I'm looking for Alouenne. Is he there?"

"Hi, is this Kabel?"

"Yes, who is this?" (Surprise to say the least!)

"You don't recognize my voice? Where have you been? I haven't seen you in a few days. This place just isn't the same without you."

"I've been on TV. I'm looking for Alouenne."

The voice on the phone said that Alouenne hadn't been seen either and people thought he and I were probably together.

"Who is Alouenne?"

When there are this many unknown elements, the evolving man does nothing. I decided to sit and muse until I felt a little more clarity. I pick up my favorite crystal. Double terminating about seven inches long, Madagascar Quarts, a few rainbow inclusions, it's spectacular. It has never let me down yet.

As I hold it in my hands, turning it and turning it, the first thing that occurs to me is, the nap, that I took a nap, is the dream. I dreamt I took a nap. It's the only dream, in the ninety days. Well, the only "dream" the way I used to use the word.

One thing is for sure. In all the history of man there has never been an authenticated sighting of a dream body by a waker, not without tons of equipment. Never, it's the Holy Grail of military dreaming.

I'm definitely there, dreaming those doctors, yet I'm at the same time physically in this house, on this couch. For the last three months, dreaming my waking side life, and every body sees me and buys me as me. Which, except for the fact that, I am, my dream body, its perfectly true.

Who have I been? Who has been living my life? A me, a total me, a me that I don't remember. A me I don't know. But how could I forget? What have I been up to? Talk about not being able to remember your dreams, what about not being able to remember your life?

Chapter Nine

This whole thing started around the time of the show. It's a very strange memory, talk about remembering a dream. I remember feeling someone get hurt. In their dream, it's so long ago. I'm in a battle. There is an Alien, no a future man, no a woman, it is changing into a beautiful blue green sphere. I'm right next to this person...

This person is so unusual, so balanced, a grace. A sphere in that color seems so natural. It just suits them. Something is interrupting the dream. The sphere is just sucked out of the dream-stream of consciousness. It seems like a weapon has been fired. Weapons, now here is my field of expertise.

The one that is so hurt? What is the name? Johnnie, Johnny? Jony that's it Jony Quixon. I remember now, the hermaphrodite that got the waking sickness. Something happened that night, during the show. Jony's has had it ninety days also. I woke up to having been asleep all this time, I wonder if anything is happening to Jony.

A local Hospital, St. Self-Esteem, provides accommodation for people with this malady. Room 2160 in fact. The room number really made me curious about whether or not some sort of clock had gone off.

As I come in the room, a doctor is attending a single patient. A frail figure sits in a comfortable chair. A few monitors pulse, etc. otherwise uncluttered as hospitals go. Silence… According to the nurse on the floor, Jony hadn't closed her eyes once in all this time.

I stood there staring at those eyes transfixed. No movement what so ever. A life of just sitting and staring. Humm… Waking traumatic stress syndrome, Yes. I'd seen something like it in Dream troops. This is by far the worst. To just sit for this much time. Almost always they come out of it in a few days. A lot of the time they start returning to normal in a few hours.

Looking at her… Wait a moment. The thin figure seems to be in a slightly different pose. It's like all the code describing her image gets re-written in sort of a wave. This is like dancing corpse phenomenon. I look away and then look back. The legs are in a different place. Am I dreaming? No. Something is sure coming over me. The two of us make eye contact. Jony stands up and walks over to me and we embrace, as two who have been in battle together.

A number of unusual things occur in this moment. The most out standing one is that Jony's body never got up. The entire time I could see the figure that was sitting there when I came in. Jony's body did not move. Not even a muscle twitched.

What else that is unusual is that I didn't move a muscle either. I thought about reaching out to embrace my comrade. There is an odd sensation. It's like some part of me breaking free, for the first time. I never move my physical body. Yet I think of doing it. Just as I normally think of moving, but it's like the muscles never get the commands from the brain. All of this happens in front of me, like I'm watching it on three separate screens at once.

And yet, a third thing that is unusual about this moment is that, Doctor Orington notices nothing. Even when I made an involuntary sound to greet Jony, he sees me just standing there, no embrace, no movement. Certainly nothing of Jony's activities appear to be registering on his sensors.

Oh and just one more unusual thing, I'm looking at Jony's dreaming body, as plain as I can see the doctor. Standing here right next to me. And I can see through it, if I desire. At the same time I can see her sitting in the chair. And to think, I came here for answers, ya right. Just more questions, a lot more questions.

I decide that, at least for the moment, not to let the Doctor into my confidence. I remain standing there mindful of his presence, while I speak with Jony. If we were two wakers, I'd properly say we were communicating telepathically. But between Jony's and I, it's more like dreamese.

We decide that it's awkward with the waking doctor in the room. We cannot truly converse. Jony tells me about a place we've been hanging out. We've been hanging out? Pardon me, We've been hanging out?

Much to my surprise, we are also known at the Dreamy Time Club. I get around. I have the feeling, I seriously get around. Maybe, I have a diary somewhere. I can catch me up on me. What am I doing? My life has just not been the same since that show.

I am about to say so long to Dr. Orington. Jony and I are shaking hands. Jony, for no reason, yanks my dreaming body. Just pulls it right out of my waking body and slams me on the floor.

I didn't know it was possible. It was such a shock to be so blatantly separated like that. And with no warning. I'm telling you, I'm a woman who holds a generals rank in a dream army. This little prank, really makes my dream ass smart.

The shock from the experience causes my physical body to faint, or more correctly falls asleep, instantly, standing up. It just looks like I faint. The moment this happens, my dream body vanishes. More correctly, the dream body jumps back in the physical body. This time however, the doctor does notice.

He goes nuts. From his point of view, he sees me go narco-leptic right in front of him. To say the least, this is embarrassing. It takes hours to get out of there, every test, gad, gag and good god. I finally just leave.

Chapter Ten

Right this way the maîtred˙ says to Jony, as she is escorted all the way to my table.

Oh finally, "Hi Jony I'm over here."

The minute the she sits, there is the waiter, just like that.

"This place has the worst service I have ever seen. I know for a fact, I have been sitting here for half an hour, not even a glass of water. Its like no one sees me."

Jony says, "Oh yes, they see you. They just don't think that you can see them. Waking people are not able to see us. So they ignore you. It's a class thing."

"What do you mean?"

"These people know that this is your waking body. They are discriminating against you. Ok, once more, they are ignoring you to get even for all the times, that wakers don't see them. Never mind."

A tall, thin, aristocratic black man comes from the back of the club. He is dressed in something that looks like a cross between a karate gi and a double-breasted silk suit.

"Kabel, may I introduce you to a friend of yours, Alouenne."

"Hello, nice to meet you, finally. I understand we already know each other. I'm still adjusting to the idea that what I'm looking at is a dreaming body. Wow, I sat here for half an hour thinking all of you are waker people. Alouenne, if this is your dreaming body, where is your physical body?"

Alouenne's is about to answer when Jony interrupts. "Alouenne is sort of grandpa. He is the very first of us, to start to walk in dream body, amongst the wakers, that is. He founded the Dreamy Time Club. His corporal body is on his boy hood home, the Island of Epiphany, with his mother."

Alouenne visibly squirms, under Jony's purposeful words. Then he speaks, "I was in the original graduating class of Integrating Astral Matrix University. Several of my graduating class got the sleeping, or the waking sickness. The first few of us could see each other and started to hang out together, even though our bodies were thousands of miles apart.

Gradually there became more and more of us. Sleeping sickness or waking sickness one thing is for sure, there are more and more of us. In a way we are all separated from our waking bodies permanently."

There are two others sitting at our table. "These are our latest two members. Red Jaguar and Clue Houstrum. We all have numbers, its chronological, Red is in at 165, and Clue joins as 166.

As founding father of The Dreamy Time Club I Alouenne, offer you General Kabel Newstarr the honorary membership number 197."

"I am both honored and an Honorary. What do we do here in the Dreamy Time Club?"

"Well tonight you are the guest of honor. Tonight, you get to be here twice, and both at the same time.

In a few moments you will be given a second Honorary Membership. Thus being the first member to hold dual memberships."

Now all of this, I'm understanding, up until this last concept. What happens next does take me by surprise. Totally, did I mention Totally? Totally by surprise eh?

Alouenne announces, "Kabel Newstarr come on out, meet the real Kabel Newstarr." A spotlight is focused. Out from a curtain comes, well, me. I'm even wearing the same outfit. Down to the last stitch.

How can I describe what I'm seeing? I walk out from the

curtain and see me looking at me. No matter where I look I'm looking at me looking at me.

I can't believe it. When will I stop saying that? When will I remember not saying that? Wait, I will remember not saying it.

I look down at my hands. I look at the other set of hands. My little cascade failure light goes off. Ahhh, No problem I'm thinking, I've been preparing for this all my life. It's simple. I am just expanding my consciousness parameters to include the two points of view at once. It's easier when you are a child, but anyone can do it.

It's like one bigger me, I am actually conscious in both places. I can see from either point of view, or both. As I learn my new consciousness, I can maintain seeing, from both views, at the same time, for longer and longer periods of time. It reminds me of when I first train to keep both halves of my brain on, while I'm asleep.

It takes some getting use to. Balancing between the two consciousnesses requires some adjustment. At first I am feeling that my dream self has been up to things my waker self wouldn't do. Oh ya. Turns out, Oh Ya. I was trashing me all over town but in a kind and loving way. Well, lets just say I did some things I would only dream of doing.

In our, and by "our," I mean my, and by "my" I mean my new relationship with myself. I, we, I agree to harmony and balance. In order to accomplish this, we agree that we forgive me all over. I feel mighty, I feel united, I feel in true harmony with the universe and myself.

The two mes, (that's mes, plural of me) the two mes look into my eyes. As thought mirrors could lend the same effect. Simultaneously I say, "So you're the real me, Kabel Verite`?"

Chapter Eleven

My waker and my dreamer both sit at the table. Jony and Clue talk bout how impressed they are with how exactly alike my selves are. Clue says that in today's society it would be unlikely that both sides of one individual could be so identical. Usually the person's self image is far different from the way they appear to everyone else. This distortion would have to have it's tell in the dreamtime body. That's unless one is purposely projecting some other, totally different, form of dream body.

Red suggests that virtually every dream body in this room is in one way or another enhanced. Augmented, by its owner's personality. I know my dream body has more height and muscle mass than my waker body, absolutely. Everyone, laughs.

Alouenne speaks for everyone when he asks, how I could

possibly project such an authentic version of my physical body, in my dream consciousness?

"All right, I'll tell ya, but I don't want you to laugh, it's so simple." This reaction, fans the flames of the latest mystery in the Dreamy Time Club, ah, myself. I paused making sure everyone would hear.

"I'm a natural, this is the answer. It's simplicity itself. I am absolutely happy with who I am, what I do and the path I'm on. I'm totally ok with me."

Jony asks me, "How can someone who doesn't know me, tell me apart?"

I say, "Alright I'll tell ya, but Jony, first I got a question for you."

"Oh ya, what's that?"

I look her in the eye and ask, "Why did you pull my dreaming body out of my waker like that? What is the matter with you? Dream body slam me, right in front of that waker Doctor that way? I was there for six hours."

"Oh… I thought you like the horseplay. What's the matter do I embarrass you, little me?"

"I admit, looking back on it, it was fun. Alight, I'll tell you how you can tell the difference between my dreaming body and my waker body. The difference? My waker is right handed. My dreaming body is a southpaw."

Clue chimed in with, "Does this mean you are ambidextrous when you are in both places at once?"

"OK, actually yes. I'm sure that's how DaVinchi did it."

The table talk takes on a more serious tone when Jony says, that there was a definite feeling of being artificially drained during the dream match. Like being caught in an eddy in the ocean. She talks about dreaming a coach having one of the doctoral staff inject something into her system during the moments before she woke.

The moment of the awakening, turns out to be the beginning, of the waking syndrome. Jony spent the next three hours, after the show, not quite awake. She talked to the officials about fowl play, just before she never blinked again.

This makes us all more suspicious, other people with a more recent membership start to question memories of possible treachery on the parts of beloved and close Dream Team members. The IG relationship is held in the deep of trust of inner human bond. It's a sacred institution.

Red and Clue are both talking about remembering having taken an unusual nap. It was about a ten-minute nap that seems to go on for days, on the afternoon, before they fell to the sleeping sickness.

A few hours, of discussion and the consensus of opinion, points to sinister, intentional, assassination regime. There never has been any accidental sleep syndrome. The contestants are regularly attacked and no one, knows it but us. But why? These people often rise to the rank our greatest humanitarians. Who would purposefully destroy, the most noble of our race?

Red asks what could be the reason? Someone doesn't want the triangular ocean, Jony was supposed to dream for them. He answers his own question.

All of the pieces drop into place as though a dream body conceiving itself. Many people throughout the world would no longer have to fish the oceans of our planet. They could heal. The planet could be fed from a triangular ocean, but a lot of people would loose a sense of self, all right, not to mention the effect on the economy.

"People being put to sleep to prevent progress? How medieval. Who could even consider such a thing?" Alouenne spoke.

Clue answered, "Well, it's been my observation that there are basically three things in the universe. First there is a huge lump of sort of a gray mass middle, the neutral part. This is by far the largest individual amount. I'm sure it would just sit there were it not for external forces working on it.

Then there is a second part that just loves to get that middle, of the line mass moving toward well, betterment, joy, happiness, fulfillment, is short a pro-evolution group.

Finally, there is that last part, that does it's level best to, in any way it can, slow everything, to slow it all, as much as possible. I believe we have run into a nest, of slowing it down obsessionists.

Kabel, can you train us so that wakers can see the dream body? Then we can expose this treachery. And Get the Dreamist off the air, exposing it as tool that is falling into the wrong hands."

I spoke, "The Dreamist Show can be, a healthy alternative, to the urge to compete that eventually became the dreaming wars. Our race acknowledges the place of evil in the universe. The idea is to honor war, the very idea of war. With the Dreamist program we pay almage to war, by having it be transmuted into entertainment. In this way, the beast of war is chained."

Red spoke next, "The secret weapon, that finally brought peace in the dreaming wars is, believe it or not, ratings. The numbers of people tuning in to broadcasts on the war significantly dropped off. The combining of the power of this many individuals, placing their attention on any subject, will make it grow. As soon as people stop placing their attention on the dreaming wars, they became history instead of making history.

As these armed conflicts wound down around the word, people started to place their attention, no longer on the wars, but protocols, etiquette, the real potential of dreaming. This is the point at which our world initiated the "Planetary Dreaming Index." This is basically a graphic analysis of the potential that dreams have to manifest in our waking reality. For example, the media may suggest that everyone who is in their fifty-second year, enter a certain code in their dream journal. Let's say we ask this group to dream rain to end a drought. If it rains there is a positive index. It would increase in relation to inches rained etc.

We then created the Dreaming Commission, which puts a halt to abusive dreaming. You have a night mirror, no problem. You intend to give some one else a night mirror, or influence someone else by dreaming, big trouble. The frequency of the entire planet went up and peace spontaneously broke out everywhere."

"Or did it?" I asked, "There seems to be a rather ominous hand at work behinds the scenes. Let's do something about it. Let us once again, hear the battle cry and this time, dream peace, instead of wage war."

Chapter Twelve

My attention spontaneously places itself on the main doors of the Club. It is lovely and ancient, blond oak wood, double door. Its windows are beveled glass, the style of whatever time period it comes from. I'm thinking, doors in dreams. This is a code, if I've ever seen one. I didn't choose to place my attention on the door. Someone else has command of the dream…

Suddenly the door just burst open in an explosion. It throws shards of glass and pieces of wood into the room. It's instantaneous chaos. Now dream soldiers all dressed in their ash gray uniforms flood the entrance to main room of the Club.

These are dream troops, unlike any I have ever seen. They all have colt six shooters. Who is in charge of these clowns? General Patton? Who would bring a projectile weapon into a dream battle? Where do these guys get these ideas?

Shots, They just begin firing. Some of us retreat back to our first bodies. Those of us who don't, witness a grim cruelty.

Red, on my left stands up. Both hands in the air, obviously surrendering, a smile on his face, they just shoot him down. Maybe twelve bullets hit him before his dream body vanishes. The guns just keep on firing.

The sound is horrifying, Jony sees Red get hit, and it happens right next to her. We are getting cut down in order. Another shot hit Jony in the hip. Impact swings her around, full face to the advancing troops. It's like a meat grinder. Little explosions occurred all over her chest, the abdomen. Riddled right in front of me. The sight of it, I could barley inhale! I'm next. I'm about to die.

Breathless, suddenly bullet holes are appearing across my chest. Three are firing at me. I hear the bullets impact my body and then hear them hit the wall behind me. Blood goes every where. The moment is as deep as shock gets.

Everything slows. I go into a flash back. It's the first day I am in basic training. My Sergeant is yelling at me because I am so naïve, that I think my job would be to dream bullet holes into the enemy. The Sergeant demonstrates how ridiculous the concept is by, shooting a hole in his own hand. I watch the bullet go through. I hear the pop from the barrel. I see the hole appear in the barracks roof. The Sergeant's hand is unaffected.

He makes me look closely at his hand. When I do he slaps

me across the face and says, "What you see in a dream, is what you 'think' you see. You are here in my outfit to learn how to 'think' differently. And your going to start here and now."

So naturally, right about now, I am wondering, how these guys are firing bullets into everyone I know. How is it, these weapons work? The fail-safe goes off. I remember I've lost command of the dream. Who is dreaming this?

My waker self is watching me from under the table. The dream bullets are having no effect on her. I can see the horror in my own face. My waking self sees my dream body being shot and bleeding.

This is my Dream! I claim my dreaming power. I feel every thing stop for a moment. All the poles have to shift. Time itself stops, while all the command codes change. The bullet holes just close. Disappearing, because I believe they are not real. The part of me watching from my waker heaves a sigh of relief. I watch me transmute my dream body. The wounds disappear completely.

Clue has been stepping backward most of this time. Her little, "don't shoot me, I'm invisible dance." Still, she looks a little tense. We make eye contact. I tell the hermaphrodite that the bullets are not real, do not believe them. Do not believe that you are wounded, no matter what you see or feel. Know you aren't wounded. It's a lie.

Long graceful wings spring from my back. Truly elegant

purple feathers lift me off the ground. The solders all concentrate their aim on me, but their bullets all go right through me. I am instantly drawing most of the fire. My strategy works, the break allows most of us to vanish through the walls. That is most of us.

Alouenne gets hit in the right bicep. Again I hear the bullet impact the wall behind him. I see him look very surprised, as he looks at his arm, involuntarily falling to his side. Then he just vanishes. Every atom in orbit in Alouenne's dream body simultaneously vibrates into another dimension. It all drops, just like the dream bodies in the holo-simulator at the studio.

At this exact moment, the right bicep of his waking body explodes. In the late afternoon, in that part of the planet, the tropical air of his resplendent child hood home, is pierced by the screams of Alouenne's mother.

Her name is Galala, she never gave up on her son. As the dreaming raid happens in the Club, as that bullet is in flight, she is sitting next to his bed reading to him. His arm moves violently, suddenly. She is instantly, covered in a spray of her son's own blood. There is the sound of the impact in the wall. She screams. This brings his other siblings into the room.

The shock wakes him up. Alouenne is awake. For the first time in many years, he is awake. His dream body finally reunited with his physical body. He walks amongst us once again. All right Alouenne welcome back! Evidently he believed the bullets were real.

So real that, in fact, there is a bullet hole, through the wall behind the bed. He will spend some time during his convalescence strolling in the garden, looking for that bullet. I guess bullet wound and the hole in the wall isn't real enough for him. If he can just find the bullet, then he can believe it. In seven years his five-year-old son will look through that hole and see the full moon.

Meanwhile, He is medivacked to the larger island where a hospital is standing by to operate. Fortunately it's only a flesh wound. The bone remains intact. And, Oh-Ya, does this make the news!

Alouenne is in line for a lot of press! Not only is he the first person to wake up from sleeping sickness. He is also one of four who get spontaneous bullet wound affect. At least this is what they are calling it. The cases occur all over the waking world. They are reported in, within minutes of each other. It's all over the planet.

These four individuals have some things in common. They are all graduates of Integrating Astral Matrix University. They all hold the title of Dreamist, and they all are people who have the sleeping sickness. What is really not common knowledge is we were all together the Dreamy Time Club, during the raid.

Chapter Thirteen

Sangik, the mystery writer, left a message for me. Apparently he knows all about the Dreamy Time Club raid. Further, he says that Clue and I had been the only ones with talent. How could Sangik know about the raid? Nice of him to notice the talent though.

I have never read a word of his works, Clue on the other hand, knows every detail there is about the "Game." Each of the twelve books stands alone as an independent unit, with its own plot and conclusion. If you successfully decode the encryption, you have successfully unearthed one twelfth of the puzzle. All twelve fit together in a bigger puzzle. Which the author calls "Greater Mystery."

Clue and I decide to meet him. I will go in my waking body.

Clue obviously ala` dreaming body. I wonder if he'll be able to see Clue?

We all meet in a waker restaurant this time. A place called The Point. How different the ambiance is in the Dreamy Time Club. This is a lovely restaurant, but, now all I hear is the ridiculous clatter of the dishes. The conversations in the background seem conspicuous compared to the telepathic talking in the Club. I am glad to eat though. I order the "Food for Thought," as my entrée.

Sangik Gibson, begins by saying hello to Clue, before speaking to me. Well at least we know he is developing his extra sensory perception. No one else in the entire place sees Clue or knows of her presence. Reminds me of being the only waker at the Dreamy Time Club.

He begins to talk about the essence of his writings. As we listen, he has been chronicling the advance of the dark forces. How they begin using, the Dreamist Show, as a way to steer the very evolution of humanity. More accurately, they would slow the evolution of our specie. For some form of personal gain they call, "Power." Like who doesn't have power?

Each of the individual novels tells the story of how certain dreamers are yanked off projects and different dreamers take their place. Then the entire project shuts down or goes in a completely different direction.

The books paint a picture of an evil spiral, originating at

Integrating Astral Matrix University. When the Dreaming Wars end, certain dreaming techniques are banished. The military publicly agrees to stop researching this type of warfare. His ideas suggest that not all is, as it seems on the beautiful campus of I.A.M.U. He believes the school is definitely the place where the troops that attacked the Club are training. Sangik, tells us he has been over every square inch of the grounds and there is no evidence of any such thing going on.

Clue and I look at each other. This points to the idea that Jony was purposefully assassinated twice.

Tell me Sangik, how does the big story end? He says he doesn't quite know. Apparently he wrote the ending to the last book and then over nights the manuscript to the publisher yet, docs not remember doing it. The publisher calls him the next day to say, he loves the ending.

I make the decision to move my waking body to where Clue's physical body is dwelling. What a complicated decision. I could dream my self their in a twinkling. What a hassle to have to fly to Clue. I really will see us be a formidable dreaming force.

While I'm packing, I see Alouenne in the media, getting off a great salvo. He explains to the world, how a dream assassin has been sent to kill him as well as other Dreamists. The fact that the bullet came into third dimension is precedent setting.

His interview spark hours of speculation as to weather or not this is an act of war. Is this somehow, some kind of war on the Dreamists? Is there extra terrestrial involvement? Who is the mastermind? The media go nuts. Like that's never happened before.

With time, both Clue and I, train our selves to project a dream body, in many new forms. Clue would dream into a houseplant, a tall elegant plant with a beautiful flower in an attractive orange purple, bloom with hundreds of petals. She even gets the scent. It's posed, regally in an ornate pot, occupying a corner of a room. She grows able to hold the pose for hours.

I would dream myself as a mist, a fog, filling the room ever so gradually. At the end of a waking hour, the flower would be almost totally obscured behind my smoky vale. With enough photographs we could dream ourselves in an exact likeness virtually anyone, or anything. We begin to formulate the course that our quest would take.

A great deal of attention is focused on the remaining people with the sleeping sicknesses. Clue's body particularly so. With the exception of Alouenne, none of the others that got the sudden exploding dream bullet affect, made it. Alouenne is the sole survivor of the event.

Chapter Fourteen

Clue is dreaming that she is in her physical body, sitting in her mother's house. I am watching this. My human body is involved in its rest cycle. There is something going on here. There doesn't seem to be anyone else home. This is very unusual. I'm alarmed. The very air itself is devoid of a certain life force.

The room is oddly lit, in a blue light, making it disorienting, almost the perfect environment to disguise the dream soldiers. Clue says, she is not dreaming this. She sounds distressed. She believes, that she is trapped in her physical body, unable to leave it. It's like being tied up. I'm not dreaming this either. I'd love to know how they do this. How can they suddenly just take command of the dream this way?

It has been a vogue for some time for people to paint themselves and then stand perfectly still, in front of some patterned wall. The paint, allowing them to bled perfectly and thus they achieve, an invisibility. Those of the world's population who are, just wakers, think it's a riot. That sort of thing is easy stuff for a dream body.

Right in front of me, three men stepping forward, just as though appearing from the walls themselves. How long were they there? All dressing in the Ashley Gray look, aren't we? I'm must say they appear intent upon the destruction of Clue and myself. Six shooters? Not this time. This time they are armed with some sort of an energy weapon. I cringe.

I think we are goners. What happens next is, the one in the middle fires his weapon. That stately plant in the corner explodes. It's the one Clue uses as a model. The energy beam arks from the weapon to the plant. First it focuses at the center of the plant. It trains itself there until a certain mass is reached. Next the beam splits into two. One beam going to the top and the other going to the bottom of the plant. I'm hearing the plant scream. It's horrifying. The plant just explodes after that sound. This whole process takes a micro-moment. The beam didn't hit either of us.

Because, I get to see the weapon fired first, I know what to expect. This does turn the tide. The assassin then looks at the two of us. Pointing the device directly at me, he fires.

Timing can appear to be critical. In the moment right before he fires, I modulate a slightly different dream body. Shall we say just one moment, before that moment, I dream a shield. I project it from my solar plexus.

The field I am emitting bounces the pulse directly back into the weapon. The assassin drops it. It starts to make an alarming noise, a reaching critical mass noise. The other two train their weapons on Clue. She, still trapped in her waker body, makes such a helpless, "victimy" target.

I expand the field parameters to include Clue's body. It's a single thought. The flash bounces back directly at the dream assassins. They retreat. The three screaming weapons die down, one by one, as I stare at them.

The room settles. The life force starts to return. The sound of the last weapon fading is like the last few drops of rain, when the storm stops. The colors start to come back in again. It seems like we had been in a model of that room and now were back in dream reality, the prana and the joy with it is seeping in again.

I am grateful to hear Clue, thank me, for my presence of dreaming mind. Walking over to her sleeping physical body I ask the tall hermaphrodite to stand up. She informs me, that there is still this pesky belief, about the dream body being tangled with corporal vessel.

I said, Clue, "I'm going show you something that Jony taught me. Ok?"

I grab her by shoulders and slam her, briskly on the floor.

She looks quite shocked. Recovering her self, she says, "So you do like the sporty stuff!"

Clue said, that Jony told her all about the doctor's office. Then she looks right at me… "Seriously Kabel please tell me how were able to figure that out so quickly? From my point of view you look supernatural. With that guy pointing that thing at me, I'm sure, I'm about to end up a scrambled pile of photons. And then, the fastest phase shift I have ever seen. It seems like your shielding arrives between the time he fires and the moment the stream would have hit me."

"As soon as he demolishes that noble plant, I realize that the solder's shot missed us on purpose, intending specifically to frighten us. If he is good at this, he knows the weapon will work on us. They know gun's wont work on us any more. So they invent this elaborate drama to frighten us. The energy form that runs their weaponry is fear. Pretty funny eh? You get the Joke? If you're not afraid the weapon doesn't work. Talk about a built in bulletproof vest.

The fails-safe just pops up, better late than never. I remember the exact minute that I lose command of the dream. The default occurred when I say, 'I'd love to know how they do this. How can the suddenly just take command of the dream this way?' See? I give up command, by saying, they have command."

My attention suddenly goes to the three weapons. Something is happening. I look at exactly the same spot, where the three of them had been lying on the floor. The information, coming from that part of the floor, is significantly different. It takes a full moment, to digest, the new information and translate it in to usable brain data. Slowly it comes into focus and then suddenly becomes crystal clear. Crystal would be the correct word.

The weapons are somehow transmuting into a single quartz crystal. It's being made from three, perfectly clear, ten inch, double terminating, gorgeous crystals, just melting into themselves. They are growing or, somehow fusing together into a perfect triangle.

Each of the double terminating crystals has exquisitely formed tips. Each of the three has a different set of terminations. One of the crystal's sets, has the generator tips. This is where all six facets on the tip, are even, isosceles triangles. It's used to focus and transmit information.

The second set of double terminations are to say the least, incredible. They exhibit the Dr. Dow formation, which is where there are three seven sided faces and three equilateral triangles, arranged all in alternating position. It is a penultimate, equilateral geometry.

The final crystal has terminations, the like of which, I've never seen. There is a six-sided plane, perfectly flat, at forty-five degrees to the shaft. It's exactly like it's sliced off. This is a scrying stone, unmistakably, the six corners of the face are bordered with, time line link, faces. Who knows how many channels this thing is capable of getting.

We are not yet sure of their use of this object. What ever this device is, it knows how to interrupt our dreams. I walked over and picked it up. Understand I've had years of military dream experience, I am, all of my life, just always, a natural. In my earliest dreams, I claimed my power every time. Do you think it's easy to get access to my dreamtime? You think you just make an appointment?

I know this triangle is in my hand because I said, "I'd love to know how these people can just walk into my dreams." They are insidious, so unannounced like that, and then dream me up, down, around and every witch away.

Look at this thing. I hold it up in the air. I've never seen anything like it in all my life. How's this for positive dreaming management protocol?

Chapter Fifteen

Clue and I decide that perhaps, a more offensive postur-
ing, would serve us well. Our first stratagem is to return to
the Dreamy Time Club, the object being to contact everyone.
Together we will begin to organize into an army. We will stop
the assassins, and restore the Dreamist show.

When we arrive at the Club it's quite a shock. Clue and I,
stand in silence as we watch what is happening. What a night
mirror we see. The walls, the tables and chairs are all in disarray.
There is still blood on the walls, bullet holes all over the place.
The acrid stench of gunpowder still hangs in the air. There are
still two soldiers standing perfectly still. They look like statues.
The whole place looks like the way the Club probably looks,
right after the massacre. It's like time has stopped. Spooky just
isn't the word.

The two soldiers stand frozen. They look like they are on their way to the exit. Clue and I stand in front of them. In a few moments we realize the two figures are moving in very, very slow motion. Suddenly the first figure modulates a pulse, like a shock wave goes through it. From the toes of the feet, on up the length of the being, it begins and bursts into a radiating red light. This shock has transmuted its field. It starts vanishing, from the bottom up. The other one pulses and begins the same process.

They vanish right in front of me, slowly but they vanish. The moment the top of the head of the second one disappears there is a dimensional shift in the entire room. Some gigantic wheel has moved a cog. Its like an instant reset. All of the walls are clean again. The furniture is up, arranged. The Club has returned to an earlier time in the evening.

The detailing is simply marvelous. I can see myselves seated there, all of us. This is the earlier that evening all right. It's the moment the doors explode open. Wow what a night mirror. Bang, it's on cue.

Once again the bullets hailed. Poor Red gets hit. Jony, gets it next. Down in order. No changes. There I go drawing fire. Alouenne looks surprised. His arm catches the bullet. Dream bodies, vanishing left and right.

When I fly up in the air, the action stops. It all just freezes. Why here? It isn't the bitter end. The soldiers begin to disappear again. Clue and I look at each other. We both know that we have only a few moments before the door bursts open again. What a horrible scenes these are. Does it just keep repeating? What a place to be stuck. What can we do? The last of the last soldier disappears again.

The stage is reset again. But it's not in the same time index. It's further on, just a little. What's going on? Jony has just been hit with the last bullet. The image of me turns to my right where Alouenne is standing, as we watch it all again. The bullet that hits Alouenne is coming at him in extreme slow motion.

I watch, as the bullet hits his arm, compressing his bicep into a distorting ball. It then explodes, blood and flesh fragments in every direction. His face opens wide. His mouth opens completely, posing in a scream. His nostrils enlarge. The eyebrows all but leave his forehead. His eyes, most of all, enlarge, bulging, taking in all the information they possibly can.

The bullet then begins to poke through the other side of his arm. A little soft cone of flesh forms on the back of the bicep. Pushing out about an inch, it begins to tear through the skin. It erupts like some tiny volcano. Four, five, six seconds and the impact of the bullet hitting the wall. This cycle is different. When the bullet impacts, everything freezes. In a few moments, the Club reset back to the moment when the bullet left the gun and headed for Alouenne.

No soldiers melting away slowly anymore. We watch it

repeat again and again. Every time the movement was a little faster. Always from the point that the bullet was fired, his arm, to the impact with the wall. The sound of fire and impact almost merge together.

What kind of a dream is this? I ask Clue. Some horrible night mirror? Watching this same moment of the raid, again and again. What possible good can this do? What is this piece of the puzzle to reveal to us?

I walk over to the character of Alouenne, and yank him out of the way of the oncoming bullet. It misses, and the Alouenne comes to life in my arms. It's an astounding thing to feel. What I grab to begin with is like a manikin. The frozen template of the body, it has no life, its like a two dimensional representation of the actual person.

Clue goes to get Red out of the path of a bullet meant for him. When she yanks him towards her, Red becomes Alouenne. Just transmutes into him. The two Alouenne's look at each other. The one in Clue's arms dissolves. It just falls into atoms that slide out of this existence.

Clue goes to her own figure. She looks at it closely. Some sort of narcissistic compulsion we seem to have built into our basic wiring. When she yanked it, that's right, it also becomes Alouenne. This Alouenne dissolves also.

Chapter Sixteen

Alouenne, It's good to see you here. Holding his shoulder, to make sure that, indeed, I am making contact, with the real dreaming body of Alouenne.

What is going on here? I ask. Strangely, Alouenne reacts by becoming embarrassed. Who's dream do you think this is, he asks? This dream, this apparition, this night mirror, is his own form of catharsis. Each time he runs through the event, he can more successfully accelerate his healing. This is the real reason the dream keeps speeding up. And a real reason that people have repeating dreams.

"Allow me," says Alouenne. Snapping his fingers and instantly the Clubroom comes back to order. This is not the reset to begin the raid. There is again a feeling of harmony. Gradually the dreaming bodies of the members of our Club begin to reassemble. The room begins to feel good again, as the herd gathers. I can finally take a moment to feel good.

There is a beautiful table with a centerpiece made of Star Gazer Lilies. Alouenne, Clue and I all sit down, I ask about the fourth chair. All of us again spontaneously place our attention on the same doors that exploded, starting the raid. This time they open gracefully and in walks in an aristocratic middle-aged Oriental gentleman. Alouenne introduces Dr. Ming, explaining that he is a Dreamist form the future.

This is not the first time Dr. Ming has been a guest in Alouenne's dreamtime. Dr. Ming talks to us, explaining that, the Dr. Ming, the Dreamist from 2160, who is all over the media, helping us to dream up time travel technology, is not the Dr. Ming talking to us now. Actually he's the great, great, great, grand child, of the 2160 Ming. Meaning that he is from a time further distant in the future.

In this future civilization, the quality of consciousness, of the average person is quite different from our time period. The information he brings us profoundly changes our vantage point of the Dreamist situation.

Dr. Ming draws a picture of the Dreamist's growth through time. He describes it as a flower that goes through many petals. It has already been corrupted by dark side, at the event of the first outbreak of sleeping sickness.

The Show's motto is true, "Before it can be, it must first be dreamed."

Before the conscious development of our dreaming power united humanity as a whole, we didn't have a very high dreaming index. Anyone could dream anything into existence. There were no standards. We are becoming ever more enlightened as a civilization. The job of dreaming, as a quintessential building block, of any creation, is done by experts. Dreaming as the first step in any creation is becoming more visible in fact, it's common knowledge.

The Dreamist's glamour, provides darkness the perfect opportunity to lure the world's great dreamers. Then they can be selectively killed or debilitated. The acceleration of our society, the evolution of our kind, has been measurably held back by the assassinations.

The Good Doctor goes on to say that, the world's triangular ocean would be existing much sooner, if Jony hadn't been killed. This ecological blessing finally does come to exist, but almost seventy-three years later. Even then it still takes another five years to get it functional. We begin to understand the reality of how, the ripples from this event radiate, on into the future.

The time has come for the show to go through a shift. We will act before anything else can prevent it from happening. Together, we will assist the production of Dreamist, into a new and evolving form. It will remain competitive, though these dark ones will no longer institute chaos. In the new show the winners of the title will be known as Dreaminaries. Those present in this room will all participate.

Ming brought some toys from the future. Twenty-sixth century dreaming knowledge must be really exciting. The doctor produces a case. It's a cube. Light gray, no handles or latches it just appears as Dr. Ming's arms seem to open some sort of portal in the air right in front of him. He lets go of it and it just floats there. We are about to find out, that it's not the box that is floating. Its what's inside the box that's floating.

He made a second gesture, audibly exhaling this time. The cube lands gently on the tabletop. The sound that it makes, tells the story of its enormous weight. Everyone looks at the box.

Another wave from the Ming and the cube pops open. Not like a chest with the hinge going horizontally, across the back, but vertically so that it opens more like an ancient steamer trunk, where the wardrobe is held neatly on coat hangers. As the two halves of the device swing open it reveals a clear quartz crystal ball, a good eight inches in diameter.

As the doctor removes the box, you could see the inside of the lining where the sphere normally sits. There are many visible circuit boards built in, the ball is obviously plugs into its packaging. It seems like the box houses some sort of very advanced computer and the ball fits into it like a brain.

The ball itself remains exactly where it has been, as the box is removed. It's now, floating in air just above the surface of the table. Dr. Ming explains further, that our first training in twenty-sixth century dreaming, will start with the four of us putting our fingertips on the ball.

We all locate and touch, the exact area that this magnificent sphere "asks" us to find. We begin to feel lightheaded. The dock tells us not to fight it. Next he gives us advice that coaches have given their men through out time. I'm sure it's unchanged since the very first coach and the very first player. He says, now this is an exact quote, "Keep your eye on the ball."

It's as though a pleasant little white cloud begins to fill the room, from the floor up. Am I slipping into my dreaming body? It's so familiar. I feel a more aggressive modulation. Something is building. There is a change of dimension, it's like we pop into a tunnel. There is a sense of wind and movement. There is a loud mechanical sound, gears moving metal squeaking.

Were in an ancient roller coaster. As we climb to the crest of the track and are held there motionless, the entire dreamscape changes as we begin the descent. That ball is really kicking in! There is the sensation of great acceleration.

It's very dark in here. Perhaps ten minutes pass or it seems like it. After a while there are faint lights in the distance, just when I'm getting used to the darkness. Still, we're moving faster and faster all the time. I begin to wonder just how long this is going to take. Almost immediately there is a light at the end of the tunnel. Through it we can see something. We can see some kind of a building, more of a house, must be just outside of the tunnel.

Before the car we are in, leaves the tunnel, while were in the dark, I have no real sense of time, but I definitely know we've moved a very great distance. If, we're where I think we are, we're back in time. We are outside of the old Triple Theta Frat house.

Chapter Seventeen

If I remember my high school temporal mechanics, correctly, then we have effectively gone back in time, sort of stretching the continuum like an elastic. Theoretically everything will start accelerating forward in time, faster and faster until. Well, no one is actually sure. Theoretically we could be catapulted right off the time map.

As we stand, we watch this old house grow older. At first slowly, faster and yet faster. Party after party, long hours of silent study, the comedy and tragedy of frat life races by us.

Suddenly all the activity stops, the house remains, but in a total silence. A moment later it begins boarding up, in another moment it's bulldozing to the ground. The actual bulldozers them selves were there so quickly that they seem like insects attacking a big pile of food, consuming it down to the last board.

The ground remains flat for a longer than the usual moment. Then the dorm begins to construct itself.

Again, as though being under construction by some sort of hyper insect, the building goes up so fast, that its not possible to make out any one worker. In virtually an instant it stood there in front of us. The time from the first light, on the first night, to being condemned takes less than one second. The hundred years of its existence just ripples by. From creation to demolition, it goes even faster than the frat house. We are still accelerating through time.

The new building is constructing faster than we can comprehend. From drawing table to open doors, again in the space of a blink. The new building is the most sophisticated dreaming lab ever built.

It's a cube. It's divided horizontally into twelve floors. Each floor is divided into 12 squares. Each of these squares has a pyramid built out of copper, crystals and circuits. The building is, in its essence, a neatly stacking one hundred and forty four pyramids.

Each individual pyramid houses a sleeping person(s) and thirty-two doctors, technicians and coaches. The combined dreaming index potential is incalculable. The planet itself could make its way amongst the stars, with such a crew to navigate.

As we focus on the building, time slows down. We somehow know that we are going to enter this time continuum. We prepare to go into the lab itself. The doctor tells us to be patient until we can modulate in the building's time frame. Only then, will we be able to inter it.

Ming gives us the OK. The approach to the edifice begins. We are still out of phase, just enough so that we are invisible to the people in this future time. Technicians, doctors, solders, citizens, all go about a normal day. We watch as different dramas are acting out in front of us. We continue our tour.

There are people being paid to dream sales for businesses. Rows of men in ties, lying in cots, dreaming sales. Little dream cubicles, influencing those who "don't" dream. This stuff is all completely illegal.

In other areas there are troops being trained, wearing exactly the same Ashley Gray uniform. Hey, the guys who attacked us are here, the raids are staged from the future.

We see the very three that attacked Clue and myself. They are sleeping, each holding onto one of the crystals, that make up the triangular dreaming crystal. The room is designed for three to sleep with their bodies at the exact same angles as the dreaming crystal triangle.

As we watch, a miniature sphere appears, floating over their third eye area, of each individual soldier. Inside the little spheres we can see the attack as it plays out. Each ball has the perspective, the point of view of the individual dreaming it. This guy is the one who shot Jony, look. How do we get to them? How we make this right?

Ming tells us to concentrate on the ball, even more intensely. Its like the thing, suddenly expands, it's all around us. It reminds me of how the blue green sphere captures the skull, during the games.

Inside of the sphere's "influence," we are standing in the dream lab in front of the sleeping solders. I step forward, further into this new reality and snatch, the crystals, from the three steeping assassins. I just go pick them up. It's some kind of a reflex. I just watch me do it. Where did this idea come from?

Ming is warning me not to touch anything. Suddenly there is a sensation that is all consuming. Like an elevator or a light plane diving unexpectedly only it's throughout your entire body, not just your stomach. It's as though every atom in creation just decides to move all at once. Everything suddenly starts moving in circles. The field is collapsing. We are all slamming back into the Club. Each of our dreaming bodies are spinning in clockwise circles. So are the tables and chairs. Everything, it's all just spinning.

The four of us begin to regain our selves. As we get back in our dreaming bodies the Doc explains that what I did, is such a big, NO-NO. When I disrupt the future in this way, it also disrupts our connection to it. That is why we are suddenly back here, not to mention spinning at an initial hundred and three miles an hour.

The dreaming sphere remains exactly where it had been, in midair exactly the same height as when we began the journey. I look at my hand and the the three crystals fused together into that same triangle on the way back. Nonetheless, this is twice now that I have gained this crystal in combat.

I gave Ming the triangle upon his request. The first dreaming crystal, the one that came into this reality, was transduced from the energy weapons, in phase. This is because I have dreamed it into this reality. It's therefore a true counting-coup, a trophy from battle.

The second one however, is out of phase and will soon begin to loose atomic cohesion. When this happens, it will leak any thoughts that have been experienced by anyone, who has touched the crystal, in its entire existence, or in their entire existence. Not only this but it includes both sides of the time line as well.

This would of course create quite a mess, with these thoughts entering the continuum, in whatever fractal they are most attracted to. This sort of thing has happened before. Most of us have suddenly been thinking a thought that came out of "nowhere," that makes virtually no sense. And further, recognize this as a thought, that is just not our own. These thoughts of course always appear chaotic because of the fractal distortion. In short, little useless leaks occur along the time line, like a form of pollution. They tend to clutter up the legitimate channels.

I hand the triangulated crystal to Ming. He puts it in the magic cube that houses the ball. Closing it, the box reacts. The edges of it go out of focus. The physical vibration of the cube is not really within our auditory range. However it's within our visual range. The color enriches, well beyond the retina's ability to translate. The mind is capable of understanding such richness, but only in a dream. How shall I say it? The luminescence increases as the box goes from red to orange. The orange grows ever brighter in syncopation with Ming's breaths. His mouth opens with a sharp sound, I'd say on the note D, the contents of the box disappear. Zip back to the future. The box cools down with in a few moments.

Ming tells us that he sent it ahead to, his great, great, great grandfather. He lives in the same year that particular trident exists, so it arrives stable. Still, it feels good to have done what I did.

Chapter Eighteen

Ming explains more about, the how and why, of what we saw in that future. "From the cave, our specie has created itself, as divided into societies. In the past there have been secret societies that have run the world. In a developing society this is normal, but only in the beginning. Then the race simply outgrows it. It turns out that this is all part of a plan for us to grow tolerance.

Can you imagine a world evolving to the point that, each citizen is sovereign with in themselves, so totally in the, "I am," as to be self governing? Each of us requiring no form of external governing, no supervision is necessary. No standing army exists for centuries. The last policeman dies at one hundred and eighty, with a zero arrest record. Well imagine it, because such worlds do live in our galaxy.

Elitism exists as long as a society is tricked into believing there is some sort of lack. Watch it happen, right before your eyes. Here's how it works."

Ming asks us, if we think that the one hundred wealthiest people in the world know each other? I think, that it's a big world and how is this really possible?

"Indeed they know each other. Who do you think, they do business with? Who do they marry their kids to? They have known each other all of their lives."

Ming says, in his future, there have been a number of us who have dreamt back in time and begun a campaign, to get the doings of these individuals exposed and defrocked.

All the wealthiest people knowing each other! This is the grandmother of all conspiracy theories. He goes on to say, that the latest incarnation of such a secret society, the one that runs virtually everything, is alive and well. Basically they are slave masters, still intact, functioning as though it were the days of Ancient Rome.

"Before we created our beautiful, One World Government, the darkness argued amongst themselves. Armies were sent marching, thousands of lives lost, to do no more than settle an argument between two schoolboys that are having a fight. It was cruel, to pretend that our planet is divided into countries. There are no countries, just family fortunes. As we evolve, we are outgrowing these immoral elitists. Fear is a fraud that's perpetrated upon evolving races."

Even in the advanced time that Ming comes from, there is still this processing. To live a life in the pursuit of joy is our birthright. If one of us is enslaved then we are all enslaved and therefore living on a slave planet. As a being of consciousness, our race is as free as the least free amongst us.

"In order to be successful, in order to defeat the darkness, we must enter the dream of my beloved ancestor's evil dreaming double. This will prove us worthy opponents, even to be able to gain access to his codes. He is the lynch pin of the Dreamist assassinations. We must find this evil one and expose his identity. Once we see his face, look into his eyes, he will no longer have any power. I guarantee you, this will be a most treacherous dreamscape, as you'll ever encounter.

The dreaming sphere that Ming brought, has returned, patiently watching us, just floating in the air, undisturbed. The four of us again place both our attention and hands on the extradimensional device.

At first it's cool on my skin. The cooling sensation disappears. Somehow the skin almost attaches to the surface. My palm adheres. It's the feel of the currents of interdimensional energy, as they begin to flow between the realms. Ming tells us this is eathertronic energy. Then he says, take three breaths, visualizing white light flowing down in a column all around us.

The ball seems to hum in my hands as I visualize this intensity of light. To look into the sphere, is to see possibilities.

As the sphere modulates the realities together we are able to see a figure inside the ball. Ming explained the orb is tuned into a possible/probable future. The actual future cannot possibly be what we are witnessing in the ball, but it may be very close.

The figure is now with a lot of others dressing in the same way. They are all wearing gold medallions with the same symbol in it. They are some sort of society. The original figure has now become indistinguishable. We watch their meeting as one begins showing diagrams of the triangular Eighth Ocean Project. The leader paints the same symbol over the ocean map in some red ink. There is a clamor of approval, laughing.

Those naughty de-evolvers. The four of us again place our attention upon the dreaming ball. The orb begins to take on a deep red color, it didn't do this before. It's the same red that matched the ink on the map. Ming says to count thirteen breaths. The ball becomes a brighter red as the number of breaths increases.

Somewhere around the fourth inhale, orange hues start coming out of the deep, the very center of the ball. Breath number seven, ushers in the full yellow. By breath ten, I am expecting the yellow to go toward green, but it doesn't, it just gets brighter yellow. On the final breath, thirteen, it winks a white flash and we are standing here, in the future... I think.

Clue, Alouenne and I all assemble our dream bodies. Little eddies of dust roll up around us, leftover mass from the time re-vectoring. We're standing pretty much the way we were at the Club back in 2097. Ming, not so much, No Ming, Mingless, as such. Where did he go? Where Ming?

Perhaps, I mean, where are we? The three of us stand, in the mega-center of an enormous square room. It has perhaps twenty-foot cathedral ceilings, all done in an exquisite Rococo. It feels ancient. Something has been using this place for a long time. Our feet stand on, a disk, one with a geometric form inlaid, just like in the show. I believe it acts like a landing pad here in the future.

If I were a detective, looking at this room, I would think I'm in the dark ages, in a place used for ritual, a sepulcher. Where is everybody? When we looked in the ball, the entire group was assembled here, in this very place. How did they leave so fast? Or is this even a question to ask?

We begin by looking around. There don't appear to be any windows. There are however, an abundance of doors, four in fact, one on each wall. The first door, the door nearest us has a large red letter E. East, Entrance, Exit what does E stand for?

Another thing that's out of place, is the fly. The common house fly, per se, just one. In the time that, the winds from our arrival take to die down and now, I have seen this fly, landing on each of us. Its like it rode in with us.

Yeah me too, says Alouenne, only the fly I see has a huge black body, more like a horse fly, not a common housefly. Clue sees an emerald fly with green eyes and body. Clearly we each see a different fly. That's assuming there aren't three flies.

Now this is clever, a second fly has joined the party. Oh boy two flies, no waiting. What is going on. We look at each other with, lets call it, a group Oops. A third fly, fourth, lets just say many flies. We went to the door marked E. Locked. We run straight across to the Door marked W. Again we find it to be locked. Now huge numbers of flies, they are starting to be obnoxious about it. They're landing on any exposed skin constantly.

We do this fly, dance, on to the final door. May I suggest, that the fly presence is approaching critical. I feel flies digging their way up my nose. I hear and feel them in my ears, they are invading my clothes deeper and deeper. I see the door marked S. Keeping them out of my eyes is a full time job. Did I mention the biting? May I say OUCH.

Fail-safe? No still hasn't fired. Oh, well. What does happen is that I have a flash back. I'm in battle. The whole trick is to recognize the enemy is disguising a door somewhere in your dreamscape. Once you rout it out, you have to get to it before, it gets a chance to shift dimension on you. You really have to think on your feet when you are dreaming.

I figure that if I'm going to hide a door in a room with four doors, a clever place would be the walls. I yell to Alouenne, while grabbing Clue by the arm. The three of us walk right through the nearest wall. Our egress occurs at a very rapid pace, Wow. Pardon me, I mean we jump through the nearest wall.

Chapter Nineteen

We enter into a place that is, well I have a very important way to describe it. This is a fly free environment. The very first thing I notice about it is, No flies, fly population is at zero. After the initial inertia, from going through the wall that fast, dies down, we find ourselves in a kind of generic ash gray continuum.

Now the fact is that, this is more of an idea-free environment, rather than just fly free environment. I can figure this out because the idea of floor wasn't particularly attended to. Although, we are definitely standing on some sort of something.

Clue notices a movement in the otherwise quiet of this place. A wisp, eh? The brush of a dark cape, as something turns.

It seems only a few feet away. The three of us move toward this feeling of fleeing.

Our advance proves to work. We flush something out ahead of us. There in the shadows, some sort of smoke, it's a figure of a man, dressing all in flowing ash gray robes. I wonder if this is an officer of the dreaming soldiers. As we get closer, he gets farther.

As we give pursuit, there seems to be a spectator. They just stand there as we run by. Then two people. They look at each other. Now we are running by people who just stop to look at us as we run by. Where do these people come from? Now, what?

Gradually, there are more and more people. It starts to become difficult to get through. We loose sight of the one we are pursuing. It becomes like New Years Eve, at Times Square, in Manhattan. There is a wall to wall crowd. He just gets away from us. What a mosh-mirror.

When the three of us get split up, in the crowd, the feeling is such an overwhelming fear that, that failsafe finally goes off. I remember, my entering a dreaming default code: "Another thing that is out of place is the fly." I didn't dream no flies. Who is dreaming all this? I claim my dreaming power.

I dream the three of us standing together, here, now. Just like the re-set in the Club. I snap my fingers in the same way Alouenne did. Instantly there is the three of us, just the three of us, standing there looking at each other. No wait, this time the ashen figure, that has been so intensely dreaming our demise, is taken by surprise. He is closer this time. Again we race to catch him.

Down a long stretch, we chase. The ashen stuff kicks up as we run. It starts to anticipate us. All around us it begins, subtly, to make little walls, in the wake of the figure ahead of us. It's like the continuum is sensing our actions, anticipating us. These little curbs, training us, guiding us, and directing the path of our steps. The little walls, they get taller. Still, we're on it, in hot pursuit.

He makes an unexpected turn. No signal, nothing. A sharp right angle, and POW, disappears behind a wall that juts up, perfectly, just high enough to hide him. It's like watching a magician's cape in action. We turn the corner, to well, let's call it a surprise. Actually amazement may be more the word.

It was the entrance to a maize. It went on simply as far as the eye could see, all in that ash gray. This guy is good. He is a master level dreamer. I've never seen any thing like this, in any file, my dream librarian can find.

Now standing here looking into this maize, I have but one question. Which is not, where did old ashen pants go, No, oh no. That's too obvious. My question is, where did I loose command of the dream? I had to have a flash back, just a minute ago, to get command of the dream in the first place.

Allow me to check into the Hotel Epiphanie, just for a

moment... Ah yes, The answer to the question is. The exact moment we made the decision to chase him. It's the exact moment command of the dream defaulted. This guy is tricky. Ya, right, he's tricky. I get it! I give him the command by chasing him and he's tricky, ya. We must allow him to come to us. Male aggressive chase, does not serve us well. The female receptive attract, this serves us well. Good how do we do this?

Clue said, That's easy, just be attractive. How do we attract someone from the future? It's easier than we might have thought. Suddenly the entire dreamscape transmutes. The maize just spontaneously forms into a beautiful tropical beach. It's gorgeous. It's so perfect.

In a few moments, as soon as our initial trepidation about this place starts to fade, as we are talking about what to do, there is a deep, deep sound. Panic runs up and down my body. Can it be the bear again? It shakes the ground. We are all three frightened. Everything goes dark, like an eclipse of the sun. This enormous silhouette of a figure, head, shoulders all tower in front of us. I can't believe it. It's King Kong. This is right out of a night mirror I never had.

I would have thought that the gigantic ape would have gone for the tall hermaphroditic Clue, but no. Apparently the big monkey has an estrogen fetish. He grabs me. Being grasped by a hand, with pads on them, like couch cushions, can convince one of one's mortality all right. Damn, if I don't let out the same scream Fay Ray did. I am such a woos-woozy. Not only am I frightened, I'm humiliated, on top of it.

Clue has a fail-safe go off. She realizes our side has lost command of the dream, yet again, when I say, I can't believe its King Kong. She claims her dreaming power and immediately dreams "monkey gone."

In deed, the big ape in question does vanish, leaving instantly visible, none other than our ashen friend. Something else happens when the monkey goes away. I am suddenly, in midair, at a pose, left hanging so to speak. I can see the little de-evolver right under me.

With the rules of gravity fully in accord, in the agreed upon parameters of this particular dream. Well, quite naturally, you could see how, I get the "drop" him. In fact it can be said that I descend upon him rendering him, splat. And all this, before he gets to say a word, about that insignificant little man in the monkey suit.

The lighting starts to change. I'm seeing this long blue frequency again. Is there about to be a raid? The three of us just turn and look at the same spot the air. Clue and Alouenne are with me sitting on our new friend. This spot in the air takes on a luster. A spinning red glimmer, an orange, building, yellow, yellow bright. And before us stands the illustrious Dr. Ming.

Dr. Ming, are we glad to see you. Yes, good to see you two. Who is your guest? We sit him up and Dr. Ming pushes down the hood and pulls off the mask. I am taken totally by surprise to see the face of, Jony. Yet again, under completely different circumstances, I am here with this person, dead, in my arms. Talk about a repeating night mirror.

Ming explains that Jony is from the future to begin with. Dreaming techniques are already far advanced from 2097. As you know some one may dream that they are awake and living some part of their waking life. You know, a lucid dream. It's also possible to be asleep and dream that you are dreaming. It's in effect, a dream with in a dream. In this future place, it's common for some souls to experience what is called, dreaming squared.

It's explored by the great dreamers of this time. While developing, the dreaming body agrees to split into two. One completely clear, to be as good, as good can get. The other equally free, to be as bad, as bad can be. Dreamtime is a gift, given to us all, to explore as many options, as we would care to. Most of the time it's regarded as safe for our waking selves.

In Jony's case the whole thing got, just a little, out of hand. She had split into her two dreaming bodies. The good one comes back through time to dream the eight's ocean as her giving, to our beautiful planet.

The dark side, battles with her. The good Jony died at your side, at the hands of her own evil self. She was the dream solder that fired the shots that hit, ah, herself.

Jony is a multiple dreaming personality? Jony, a suicide, how can this be? Plus, not to mention plus, I just unknowingly splat her, like an insect? Every time I turn around, I am grieving all over again, for this person.

Chapter Twenty

Jony is not the person we are looking for. Ming explains that, the one we are pursuing is a dark Doctor Ming. He is the mastermind that is turning the Dreamist into de-evolution for hire. Alas, the one responsible is my ancestor's dark dreaming double.

Ming reveals that he's been sent back to straighten the whole thing out. Don't feel so bad about my great, great, great, ancestor's time. It was his grandmother that wrote this book and read it to him as a child. Her name is C. Ming Li.

By now, in my time, here in the twenty-six hundreds dreaming grids extend across galaxies. There is no limit to what mankind can dream.

I have come here to put an end to the slavery of mankind. As soon as I can remove my illustrious ancestor's evil dreaming double from the equation, I can strike a blow against the Dark Luminati of my time. The entire organization is built on, separation. The elitist paradigm, is technically an impossibility, simply because, what is good for any one of us, is good for all of us. The family of humanity is one family.

It's simply truth and no one can stand in opposition to it, for an extended period of time. We are all one. We are one gigantic family. There is no one on this planet to whom, you are not blood kin. Know that no matter where you walk, you walk amongst your family.

As he continues our training in dreaming abilities, he gives us each, a flat disk about one inch in diameter. One side is smooth and opalescent. The other has that familiar circuitry look, only it has much more of an organic nature. He tells us to get used to trusting our instincts about them. They are truly beautiful.

He demonstrates one by placing it on his third eye and projecting a sleeping cat on a beautiful silk pillow right into this reality. Right in front of us it's a living catnapping, au cushion. Ming introduces us to this animal, as his beloved pet. Her name is Jaku. She is an exceptional being and would volunteer to come with us, if we wished.

We'd be honored, Jaku, welcome. Ming departs and we wonder how we can find evil Ming, save the show and make the world a better place.

Chapter Twenty One

"Well let us look at this. What do we have that the Dark Ming would desire to posses? Well we can rule out me." said our tall blonde.

"Why do you day that," I ask?

"Well," she said, "He doesn't have a Clue and it seems to me, he isn't looking for one." We all laughed, just not very hard.

Alouenne says, "I know what he may desire. Jaku!"

"Alouenne, are you suggesting that we would use and endanger, the latest member of our little task force, to lure the dark one out of his dreaming disguise." I ask.

We all look at each other. Yes? Then we all agree. The cat.. is it. Provided she's willing.

How do we do this? We all three, look at the beloved

pussycat. You could actually hear the pointy eared pile of cat fur say, "You lookin at me?"

We begin to pet, stroke, scratch, rub, and tickle the little girl. Silent little purring cat giggles, went off into the air, much like the hairs form her coat.

The group of us, feeling and exhibiting this much loving, of course, gets the attention of the evil dreaming double. In the moment, between the beat of a heart appear three figures. More soldiers? The one that came from behind me is me. I'm looking at me, and this time it isn't the other me, its some other, other me. A dreaming clone. A manufactured imposter. It looks more like a model.

Not to totally, reveal the Neandertal, that lives in all of us, but my first impulse is, to take a swing at my own jaw. The clone me, easily counters my movement. Taking my arm and pulling me forward, and I'm off balance. I'm acting like a rookie. I'm suddenly looking at all this, form the perspective of the floor.

All right, it's a manufactured imposter, but it's a really talented manufactured imposter. Or is that, I am really this talented? That was me making both sets of moves? Who is kicking my ass? Am I kicking my own ass here? What is this?

The one that comes toward Clue, stands nose to nose with her. Mocking, taunting, egging-on, exhibiting the most vile sort of derisive effrontery imaginable. It's astounding what an exact copy this thing is. Every detail, precisely. It makes little howls, like a monkey-self dancing up and down in front of her.

Clue has basically the same reaction as myself. When she takes her shot, the copy Clue, catches the fist of the real Clue. The two of them take off. It looks like they dance some sort of ballet. As one advances the other retreats. Its like being matched with an opponent that is an exact copy of you, and, I said, <u>and</u>, it knows exactly what you are about to do and right before you do it. How therapeutic.

Alouenne's dreaming doppelganger comes from a different perspective. He draws a gun. It just appears. A 45 automatic, like so many other fine implements of war, it's first invented in the twentieth century. We watch as the clone fires eight shots into Alouenne.

The first shot knocks him down. He goes sprawling. Slides maybe four yards after he hits. Alouenne's dark double continues to fire. The bullets appear to impact the body. When the clone stops firing. We stand silently, looking at the figure of Alouenne on the floor. No blood...?

Alouenne? He is suddenly standing up. That is, he stands up all in one movement. Something like inch worm choreography, it's a current that goes through him that lands him standing up. Any gymnast in the world would be proud. If we hadn't been dancing with our personal clones, we would have given him a round of applause.

He later tells me that when, I pull him out of the path of the bullet that keeps hitting him, his waker arm instantly heals. No scar, as though it never happened. During the clone's assassination he is laying there, actually enjoying the experience of being shot because he knows they weren't real. Hot lead, has a different taste from this point of view. I'll tell ya, thrill seekers, there's one in every dream.

While these dreaming mirror selves are being so entertaining, perhaps distracting is more the word, the Dark one is stepping, literally, out of a fold in the air. Just his upper body came through as though reaching into our dimension. He snatches the feline. Whiskers, claws and follicles, say by-by.

Zip back into the seeming emptiness of the air between us. Gone like snow on the water. Gone and with him went our plan, not to mention the cat. How do we go on? How can we re-dream this?

Much to my surprise, to everyone's surprise, I take command of the dream. No flash back, no dreaming code default, this time it's simply by my command. Wham, the combat we are engaging in, simply stops. The shadow versions of our selves stop in mid-movement and they just remain there.

I realize that this is because I have made no decision about what would occur after I take command of the dream. They just stand frozen awaiting orders. I take a really careful look at the me. Ah, inferior materials, still it's an unusual mirror. I tell them to vanish.

I wonder, where the real Ming might be. This statement is taken as a command and so the good doctor appears, preceded by his traditional "white pop." He looks at us. So glad to see him, we tell him about the doppelganger party. From the, sweat, chaotic body language and disheveled clothing, he deduces that our encounter may not have gone as well as its potential has suggested. Then we tell him the news about the beloved feline, Jaku.

I begin to recount the details of the encounter. His eyes tell us that all is forgiven. He explains, that while what has happened, is not our plan, it's indeed his plan. He has long been training his faithful pet in telepathic communication. They have been playing hide and seek games since Jaku was a kitten. Ming tells us that the actual cat is not more than ten feet from us even though we aren't detecting her. The evil Dr. Ming is studying her, even now, to determine how love works.

How do we get the kitty back and expunge the deeds of the evil Ming from the dreaming grid? Easy said Ming, in fact this could be referred to as a piece of confection.

He tells us to place our attention on the disks he had given us earlier. We stand in an equilateral triangle around him each of us holding hands with our arms parallel with our side of the triangle.

Ming begins one of is famous breathing exercises. As it reaches its peak he claps his hands, three times. A moment later and there is an enormously loud sound. It's definitely a crash, like a sheet of glass breaking, like a thousand sheets breaking. There is some sort of harmonic with in it, another sound that makes it seem more like an implosion. Something like a vacuum implosion, like an air lock, or one of those ancient TV monitors folding in on itself.

The entire ash gray continuum, we had been battling in, disappears. Ming explains that, even the generic ash gray reality, is an idea, and that now we were in an even more "idea free zone." He cautions us not to even attempt, to draw a conclusion as to where exactly we are. If we do we'll get tangled in who knows what sort of, what he calls, "speculation."

What is un-mistake able is the sound of the cat meowing, coming from just behind Alouenne. We all turn to see the dark Ming holding Jaku. The light Ming tells us that we still have the command of the dream. He then instructs us to dream the dark one falling asleep.

Old evilness, wasn't about to take this lying down. He turns, clutching the cat close to his chest, and begins to flee. With presence of mind that is surprising to me, Alouenne manifests a boomerang. Just like that, out of the air, and by his command.

He simply sates: "Three-pound, ash wood boomerang with Dharawal tribal markings, circa 800 B.C.E."

With the skill of an Elder Bushman, he sends the weapon on a course designed to render the dark Ming unconscious.

The boomerang accelerates into its arc, with that sound that must be similar to a bird's wings. It hits its mark perfectly, contacting the base of the skull just above where it joins the spinal chord. The momentum of the dark one pushes his body forward. As the legs loose their traction, he careens forward making the entire movement into a circle. It's the penultimate, "head over heals." Well that takes care of the falling part. I'll bet he's asleep to.

Way to go Alouenne! This time we do applaud!

Evil Ming has landed flat on his back, sprawled out like a prizefighter, down for the count. The beloved feline is sitting on his chest. We three stand in a circle around him. Jaku stands up on hind legs and does literally a victory dance punctuating it with a series of cat language hurrahs. Since I am not fluent in cat, I will assume that is translated roughly, "Take that, you walking pile of nonspecific waste products." The good doctor retrieves his pet, holding her to his heart.

We have to be swift. We must do this before he has been asleep to long. His dreaming body will emerge and then we will lose our advantage. Ming tells the three of us to focus our disks on the dark Ming's heart. We do so. Jaku, climbs to a perch on Ming's shoulder. Dr. Ming, himself straddles the sleeping figure and kneels down.

Ming says, Focus your attention, I am about to rip the mask off of my sleeping great, great, great grandfather's evil dreaming double. I am warning you, that the face you will see does not have a single trace of human kindness left in it. Just, prepare yourself. We hold our breath.

He does the deed, he yanks the mask off his head...

I am expecting to see some dark likeness of the beloved Dr. Ming. Perhaps some twisting contortion of the benign features I know, but no. Before my eyes its the face of The.......I can't believe it. When will I remember to avoid saying I can't believe it?

The entire dreamscape just collapses in front of us. Everything disappears, Clue, Alouenne and I, are just sucked into the place where that face had been. It's the face of... I can't bel...i...e... v...e i....t...... All right I believe it!

A jolt goes through a sleeping figure. This is the physical body's responding to its beloved soul's return. The body takes that long grateful breath, welcoming its consciousness back to the helm. A figure is now slowly sitting up in bed.

A sleepy mind, looks down at a sleepy hand. "The Runger sure had a lot of dreams last night. I think the Runger was a Ringer."

He looks down at what's in his hand. The triangular dreaming crystal gleamed. A last flash of light glimmers through it. It's the energy still contained in it, from its transfer into this realm. Holding it up to the light…"What? What is this thing? What's The Runger going to do with this? It's pretty though."

The Runger had dreamed the whole thing. When the hood was yanked off him, exposing who he really is, it so frightens, The Runger that he retreats back to his physical body. He would have rather died than reveal who he really is. Well, really is, in this particular dream.

"One of these days, The Runger is gonna start a dreaming journal. Oh well, time to get moving, The Runger is due at the Dream Dome in three hours. Quite a show tonight, come to think of it, there is a first time ever, an x-military dreamer on the bill this evening, a woman to…"

The End

A Very Brief Biography

In 1977, Mr. Johnston experienced the death of his body after being hit by three bullets, a mugging in Manhattan. He journeyed to the other side. Extensive meetings with our Angels provided him with an expanded perspective on life, and an important mission. He, along with many others is to assist in the raising of human consciousness to the point that the advanced civilization on our planet will spontaneously appear.

Toward this end and for almost forty years, he has been assisting people to see their past lives. His teachings include: Palmistry, Physiognomy, Kinesics, Language Codes, Galactic History and Trinity Thinking. Initiations facilitated: Seichim, Opening of the Third Eye and The Ritual of Remembrance.

Neville also works with the Quartz Crystal Bowls and Tuning Forks. Since 1997 he has been dreaming and building copper crystal energy devices. In addition he is co-host of a very popular program called Telepathic TV. Just go to telepathictv.com Thursday evening at 8:30 EST. You may call in with a dream, or a question about anything.

Other Books by R. Neville Johnston

The Language Codes
Hidden Language Codes

Our speech is full of unconscious triggers. It is unlikely that we are very aware of these little land mines, either when we use them or when they are used on us. These triggers could be understood as "programs."

A program is to a computer, as a word is to your mind. In other words, if you have a word in your head, you have a program running. Think a word or say it and it activates the program.

Lets take a look at the program "problem." When one person says to another, "We have a problem." We watch this person put on a suit of armor. Sharpen their weapons and prepare to go to war. They don't know what war or how they got drafted. The program, "problem" is running. While all this is going on, nothing is going on.

Retrain your mind to hear the word symptom, whenever you hear the word problem. "Houston, we have a symptom." The symptom that the astronaut spoke of was the government not telling people what they are doing. The company that built that part of the rocket would not have made it the way they did if they had fully known what it was to be used for. It could all be so different!

A word is a decision made. Many of these words are not making kind decisions for us. While it is true that information rides on the current of words that is our speech. It's through the selection of these words that the reality in which we live is created.

These two books are lists of words that are literally killing us, and how to change the programming that is creating all this. In the magnificence that is the human mind, your mind, have you ever found the delete key, the up-grade protocols, the ability to defrag, etc.? All of this is to be found in these writings.

Eleven Self-Empowerment Protocols

New Paradigms for Our New Civilization

The protocols book is designed to get us on top of these little things that knock us down so easily. It is a teaching about becoming whole and complete within our selves. Think of yourself as self-fulfilled, self-generating, self-existing and at the same time integrated into family, friends and society.

This work reminds you to notice that you are feeling bad about something and then how to plug in a protocol and then Voila, resume carefree play.

An introduction to Trinity Thinking is the third protocol. The forth is about no longer being a guilt puppet. This is the way of the future. It's no longer about some guru, it is time to see that it's about you!

Put your life back into your own hands. The age of co-dependence is coming to a close. Classes, teachers, books, yes. Now add something more to it. Add yourself.

Obtaining These Books

They are available through Borders, Barns and Noble, <u>Amazon. com</u>, Kindle on Amazon, and through Metaphysical shops.

"Eleven Self-Empowerment Protocols," is also available through <u>Authorhouse.com</u>. as well.

Any of the books may be obtained as, signed copies, directly through the Author.

Author Contact Information

R. Neville Johnston

2210 Coppersmith Sq.

Reston VA. 20191-2306

e-mail at telepathicguy@Yahoo.com

Website at www.telepathictv.com

Or call 703-346-7430

& Thank You for getting in touch!

Breinigsville, PA USA
14 January 2011
253316BV00003B/3/P